Led Astray

Led Astray

Pat Tucker

URBAN BOOKS

http://www.urbanbooks.net

This is a work of fiction. Any references or similarities to actual events, real people, living or dead, or to real locales are intended to give the novel a sense of reality. Any similarity in other names, characters, places, and incidents is entirely coincidental.

URBAN SOUL is published by

Urban Books
10 Brennan Place
Deer Park, NY 11729

ISBN-13: 978-1-59983-030-8
ISBN-10: 1-59983-030-2

First Printing: August 2007

10 9 8 7 6 5 4 3 2 1

Printed in the United States of America

Keisha

I sighed hard and loud, then shook my head in sheer disgust. I hate to see a grown man cry. So you know the sight of my husband of five years fighting back tears was making my stomach churn and it definitely wasn't helping our current situation.

"So are you saying you want a d-divorce?" Dexter buried his face in his palms. Before I could answer, he groaned in frustration. "I can't believe I'm hearing this."

When he looked at me with such evil in his eyes, I felt like I needed to say something before things really went downhill with us. Dexter might be pathetic, but I still loved him. "No, that's not what I'm saying," I tried to explain. "It's just that—this isn't what I thought it was going to be when we got married."

"I've given you everything."

"Everything but what I want," I answered quickly.

"What's that?" Dexter asked loudly.

"You."

The house was quiet except for the faint sound of the television left on in our bedroom. I glanced around the room. On top of the maple-colored coffee table sat the vase that used to hold fresh flowers he would bring me every week. A large glass urn still contained sand from the beach where we were married. Everywhere I looked there were reminders of us during happier times. We had stained the dark hardwood floors ourselves. It had been one of those weekend Home Depot projects.

Everything about that room was so meticulous, everything perfectly in its place. The perfect room, in the perfect house, for the perfect couple, but that was only how we appeared on the outside. What we'd become inside this perfect house was something far different.

He stared up at me again, this time with bloodshot eyes. "You have me, Keisha. You have all of me," he said passionately.

"No, I don't!" I said, louder than I needed to.

"What *are* you saying Keisha? I mean, help me out here. I'm confused." I tried to reach for him, but Dexter jerked back beyond my grasp. "I need to know *exactly* what you mean, Keisha. Either you want me and us or you don't. There's no gray area here. It's that simple!" His voice grew louder. I could see the pain etched into his features, and, for a fleeting moment, I regretted even bringing it up. I wondered if I should've just continued to suffer silently.

I didn't say anything right away. I looked at Dexter, looked in his eyes and thought about why I had even fallen in love with him. I loved his gentle nature, his mild manner, his patience and understanding. It's ironic how those were the exact same things that were now boring me out of my mind.

The thrill is gone!

That was what I wanted to scream at him. But instead

I said, "All I'm saying is some things have got to change."

"What things?" he asked.

"We're in our thirties, baby, not our sixties."

"I never said we were."

"No, we just act like it," I said quietly.

"What you say?"

"I'm so tired of this humdrum life. Sometimes I'm so damn bored I just want somebody to come and put me out of my friggin' misery," I growled angrily. It was how I got each time I thought about it.

Dexter abruptly got up from the sofa. I never feared my husband, but his sudden movement caught me off guard. His massive frame now towered over mine. "Misery?" he shouted at the top of his lungs. "Is that what it's like being married to me now? Misery?" He shook his head like he was trying to make sense of my traitorous words. He was frowning, and his deep voice boomed throughout our house, bouncing off the walls and cathedral ceilings. A layer of sweat was glistening on his forehead, and veins were now bulging at his temples. Dexter's body shook as he spat his angry words in my direction.

I had never seen Dexter this upset. With his eyes narrowed, he flexed his fists, almost like he was struggling to maintain what little composure he had left. His pain had turned to anger right before my eyes and it made me very uncomfortable.

But even though he was speaking to me through gritted teeth, deep down, this shit was turning me the fuck on, because the truth is, he was finally paying me some attention.

I was getting all emotional about it.

"I work my ass off so you can live better than good.

Look around you! You have everything you want, and you're telling me you're suffering? In misery, even?" he ranted. "I guess you'd be happy if I was beatin' your ass, and cheatin' on you like that last fool you were with?" He got in my face. "Would that make you happy?" he screamed.

I couldn't believe he'd gone there. I swallowed back tears of my own, and turned away from him. After a good moment or two, I exhaled and calmly said, "Dexter, I'm not trying to fight with you. I'm just trying to let you know how I feel. Lately things have been dull. All you do is work and when you're here you never wanna do anything. It's like you've gotten way too comfortable." I sat up and ran my hands down his legs. "We're not special to each other anymore," I said in my best pouty voice. "I mean, I know your routine, better than I know anything else. It would be good if we could just, I don't know, spice it up a bit. That's all."

"Spice it up? You got your goddamn nerve!" I spun around to see Dexter's mother, Hattiemae Saintjohn, sashay into my house like her name was on the fucking deed. "You should be overjoyed to have a man like my Dexter!" her voice shrieked. She was a small, petite woman with pinched features that made her always appear angry, even when she wasn't.

I was dumbfounded by her presence. "H-how did you get in here?" I asked, still in disbelief. Her presence said I was outnumbered in more ways than one.

She ignored my question and shot daggers at me with her eyes. "That should be the very least of your concerns."

"No, you need to tell me how you got in this house!"

"With this key," Hattiemae said, holding up a key.

"What are you doing with a key to our house?" I demanded.

"I gave it to her," Dexter finally said.

"What does she need a key for?"

"In case she needed to get in." He turned to his mother. "But I didn't expect you to just walk in like that."

"You damn right she don't. She don't need a key."

"You have the audacity to talk to my son like that in his own house?" Hattiemae said, and I looked at her like she was crazy. *His own house?* "Trying to make him feel like *he's* not worthy of *you?*" she spat at me, and went to his side. "See, that's what's wrong with you new-millennium women. Your husband is home every night. He works hard to provide a comfortable lifestyle, one we all know you'd otherwise never be exposed to, and you're still not happy, ungrateful even. Then, you got the nerve to complain—hmmm, you don't deserve him." She shook her head with disdain. "Son, I've told you time and time again, I don't care how hard you try, there's no way you can make a housewife out of a whore," she said sweetly as if I weren't even in the room.

Dexter dropped his head and rubbed his temples like he really wasn't in the mood to deal with his mother or me. I fought back tears as I snatched up my purse and stormed out of the house. I needed to get away before I said or did something I'd regret. I knew Dexter wouldn't stand up to his mother for me. He never did, which was just another thing I felt caused a problem in our marriage.

I drove mindlessly around Houston, replaying the evening's events over and over again in my mind. I tried to put Hattiemae's hateful words out of my head and focus on the real problem. I was absolutely bored with my marriage.

I thought about that old marriage cliché about the seven-year itch. Well, I could tell you firsthand, that's a bunch of bullshit. I had needed scratching just a couple of years into my marriage.

I know marriage isn't easy. In fact, it's a whole lot of hard work, especially for someone like me.

When I was living the single life, I loved and cherished my freedom. I enjoyed coming and going as I pleased, partying till the wee hours of the morning or even the next day if I wanted, and not having to call and check in.

I wasn't looking for love, and I definitely wasn't looking for a husband when Dexter came along. He wasn't even my type back then. I needed the type of man who walked with a swagger of arrogance. One who was a little rough around the edges, with an air that hung above him, leaving us all to wonder whether he was really a true-to-life thug. Those days there was nothing a straight and narrow guy could do for me and that's what Dexter was.

But somehow, despite that, Dexter was different to me.

He was handsome, kind, and he was a great listener. Dexter was things I had never been exposed to in a man, so his qualities were magnified from where I sat. I may have been a free spirit, but I've never been a fool. There was no way in the world I was going to let a good man pass me by.

Our friendship quickly exploded into a steamy romance, almost like the kind of stuff you read about in the pages of those erotic novels. The sex was the bomb. It was like he worked to keep me satisfied at all cost. He did all of the right things while we dated. He even gave me time to get my old life out of my system. And trust me, that was not an easy task, but he was patient with me.

Two years after we met, we were married on a beach in the Bahamas. At the time I thought I had made the right decision, but seven days into our marriage, on the day we were leaving paradise, second thoughts started creeping up on me real fast. I started wondering, what if I had settled too quickly?

What if I only thought he was Mr. Right?

So what he'd been the only man who ever did right by me?

Did that mean he really was *my* Mr. Right?

After what I'd been through before Dexter came along, well, I was bound to fall for just about anything. Unfortunately, I was used to men who played games and sent mixed messages.

But not Dexter.

He had been clear about his intentions from day one. I especially liked the way he told me up front that he was ready to get off the market and had no intention of wasting his time or mine.

Back then I thought he was an aggressive take-charge kind of man with an assertive attitude and it had turned me on.

But lately all of those traits had all but vanished, as if they were never even there. I started wondering if I had only imagined them because I didn't want to be wrong about the choice I had made.

Not to mention, Dexter's mother and sister were about to work what little was left of my very last nerve. Couple that with him slacking off in so many areas and I'd been close to losing it.

Dexter was no longer as attentive. He barely acknowledged my presence at times. Then he spent more time hugging beer cans than me, and going out suddenly turned into a rarity, if it happened at all. And to top it all off, his skills in the bedroom had seriously slipped, and he didn't seem the least bit concerned.

Lately I'd only been surviving by telling myself, "Keisha, even though his family is certifiably crazy, and things have gotten a little monotonous in the bedroom, overall, Dexter is still a good man." That's how I had been soothing my itch, and it had been working for the most part. But I had finally reached my breaking point.

I navigated my car onto the 610 Freeway and passed the spot where Dexter proposed to me. I sighed. Dexter was good to me and for me and I knew it. He made me want to do better and be better.

Back in the day, Dexter had basically restored my faith in men. He inspired me to see what was possible between a man and a woman in a committed relationship, because before him, I had one loser after another.

So why wasn't that enough?

As I bobbed my head to the sounds of Jay Z and Beyonce crooning about déjà vu, pumping from my car radio, I couldn't help but wonder if the excitement I was feeling just from the music was the reason I was so miserable. Maybe everybody was right about me. Maybe I was a party girl who simply couldn't be reformed.

"No!" I snapped to myself. "Nobody believed in us except us," I said to the rearview mirror like it was Dexter. "Everyone said we wouldn't make it and we've been married five years." *Dexter is a good man,* I told myself. "I can do this. I will do this," I mumbled.

As I listened to Heather Headley sing about being *his girl,* I knew what I needed. Dexter had committed himself to me and worked every day to make me happy. I took the first exit off the freeway, made a U-turn, and started making my way home to my husband. I had to push the party girl inside me aside and keep my eye on the bigger picture. But even as I stepped on the pedal I knew it would be a serious challenge. I could only hope I was really up for the task.

But first things first, and the first thing on my list was putting that snooty bitch Hattiemae Saintjohn in her place, and out of my goddamn house!

Dexter

I couldn't wait to finally face the naysayers. Tonight Keisha and I would be celebrating five long years of marriage. And let me tell you something, this wasn't your ordinary anniversary. This would be the day most people never thought would come.

Everybody had something to say about Keisha and me. She was wild when we met, nobody knew that better than me, but she had changed.

Back in the day, Keisha was known for shutting down the club. It didn't matter which club, if it was jumping, you could be sure that Keisha would be there. She used to hang out with her girlfriend April. Partying for those two was serious business. We bumped into each other at Club Maxis off Westheimer, one of Houston's hottest clubs at the time. I wasn't brave enough to even attempt to approach either of them for a dance. But the longer I stood and watched her, I knew there was something about Keisha, something special.

I knew I had to have Keisha from the first moment I saw her shaking those hips. The way Keisha moved her body on the dance floor was enough to make every man in the room stop and pay attention.

And what a body it was. Keisha stood about five feet six inches tall, 145, give or take, and my baby was nice and curvy. She could've been an athlete with a body like that. She had firm leg and calf muscles, and near six-pack abs. Even after five years of marriage, I'd have to say we both still looked real good, and even better together.

I was gearing up for a mind-blowing anniversary celebration. Especially since Keisha all but told me she wasn't happy anymore. My mind was set. I needed to do something real special to show Keisha *we* were worth fighting for. The more I thought about her words, I had to admit, I had slipped down a notch or two. But all of that was about to change, and this party was going to be the first step toward change for us. Not to mention, I definitely wanted to show all the naysayers that they were dead wrong about us. Of all people, it was my friend Larry who gave me the idea of what to do.

Larry used to be the main one telling me about the mistake I was making by marrying Keisha. He had said she was "out there" too much. Larry and another friend, Roger, had come right out and told me Keisha would be too much for me to handle.

I have to admit I was probably the happiest man in Houston when April announced she was leaving with some man she met out at Ellington Field. He was in the National Guard. I knew with April gone, Keisha and I would be just fine. I'm not saying my woman ain't got a mind of her own, but I knew it was hard for her to tell her friend no.

April came back for our wedding, but by then the man she left Houston with was history. She came to our wedding with some new dude. I didn't say a word. I was just glad she was there when Keisha needed her.

Once Keisha and I settled into our nice life here in Katy, a suburb of Houston, we had what I thought was a pretty good life. I heard what she was saying about being bored and all that, but other than that, it was great. Keisha taught middle school and they were on summer break. That's why she was getting a little restless, but I'd make it up to her. I loved her too much to let her go.

I was in love with everything about my baby. It was the way she looked at me. Keisha had the biggest, prettiest smile and eyes that seemed to dance when she saw me. The way she said my name or called me "baby" drove me insane. And she was so smart. My baby could speak intelligently about anything, to anybody. Rich or poor, black or white, it doesn't matter, she was just good with people.

And Keisha was so sexy. The clothes she wore, and all that sexy lingerie she pranced around the house in— made me wanna—she was right, I had gotten too comfortable. Too complacent; I had to take care of my baby or I would lose her for sure.

I couldn't let that happen. Keisha was my world. I couldn't image a scenario where I could be happy without her. I was determined to make things right.

All I had to do was keep Mama from barging in on us. I had to take that emergency key from her. My mom wasn't shy about how much she hated my wife. She had even tried to convince me that Keisha and I might not legally be married since our wedding was on an island instead of in a church. But no matter what she said, Keisha was my woman and I loved her more than words could ever possibly express. Mama would just have to get over it.

As I pulled into our driveway, I grabbed my cell phone and dialed Larry's number. "Hey, man. Is everything okay?"

"Yeah, I'm pulling up to Hobby right now. Her flight should be here soon. Then we're off to the hotel."

"Good. I'm about to pick up Keisha now. You talk to Roger?" I asked.

"Yup. Man, it's all good. I'm about to park, so I'll holla' at you later," Larry said.

It looked like everything was falling right into place. It was six-thirty and I only had to shower and change and we'd be on our way.

I couldn't wait to see the look on Keisha's face when it was all said and done.

Keisha

I was dressed, ready, and anxious, when Dexter finally showed up. I tried my best not to be mad at the fact that he still had to shower. After all, it was our anniversary, so I remained quiet and exhaled as he handed me two dozen long-stemmed roses and rushed into the bathroom.

"Honey, I'll be good to go in ten minutes," he said hastily.

I rolled my eyes at his back and took a deep breath, inhaling the roses' sweet scent.

"You got ten minutes!" I shouted for good measure. He had me so curious about his plans. I couldn't imagine where we were going for the evening. But I was glad he had taken our little talk seriously and was obviously trying to spice things up a bit.

When I got back to the house the other night, thank God his mother was gone. At this point, I couldn't really say what would've happened if I had to put her nosy, meddling ass out. But trust me on this one, I was ready and prepared to do just that.

With Hattiemae being gone, it gave Dexter and me a

chance to talk. I took back some of the things I said, you know, like me being so bored that I just wanted somebody to come by and put me out of my misery. Yeah, I had to apologize big-time for that one.

We sat and talked until almost four in the morning. Maybe I was just starved for attention, but it felt so good just to talk again. After a while, I curled up next to him and rested my head against his chest. Dexter wrapped me up in those strong arms of his; and I was in heaven. Somewhere in all that, Dexter and I agreed that we would try to work things out.

When my man strutted into the family room exactly ten minutes later dressed to the nines in a chocolate pin-striped suit, I nearly fell out, he looked so good. I stood up right away.

"Dang, baby, you look like brand-new money! Turn around, let me see you." I stepped back to get a better look. I knew the suit was new because I hadn't seen it before. Dexter had his fade haircut just the way I liked it and his goatee was freshly lined. His mocha-colored skin glistened. I hugged him and inhaled the strong scent of his Cool Water cologne. When I stepped back, he started styling and profiling for me again. "Man, you better be glad you're already spoken for," I teased.

"Yeah, somebody already has papers on me," he sang as he turned again to his left, then to his right, striking a serious pose.

I looked at the clock. "Okay, it's ten minutes to seven," I warned.

"Oh, yeah, that's right." When Dexter reached into his pocket I didn't know what to think. My heart nearly stopped, but I tried to play down my excitement.

"You look so beautiful, Keisha." He took me into his

strong embrace. "You're more beautiful today than five years ago."

"Don't make me cry, I'm gonna mess up my face, babe." I frowned a bit when I realized what he pulled from his pocket wasn't a box of jewelry, but a blindfold.

"Okay, do you trust me?" Dexter asked.

I nodded.

"Good," he stepped toward me. "I'll need you to put this on once we get into the car. I need you to keep it on until we get to our secret destination."

"Why do I have to be blindfolded?"

"You said that you trusted me," he said and stepped close to me.

My heart started racing. "Yes." *Make-up sex is everything it's said to be.*

"Then trust me. Can you do that?"

"Yes." I could barely contain my excitement. When he handed me the blindfold and one of my sleeping masks, both of our hands were shaking. For the first time I felt good about the talk we had. I started feeling like he took what I had said to heart. He was giving me a double shot of spontaneity and excitement. Just as I prepared to turn and walk out of the door he stopped me with his hand.

"Oh, before we go, I have something special for you," he said.

"Oh?"

He reached into his pocket, this time his breast pocket, and pulled out a long velvet box. I gasped when I opened it and saw a sparkling platinum diamond tennis bracelet.

"Oooh my . . ." I managed.

"I love you, Keisha. You deserve this and so much more. Here's to five more to the tenth power, baby."

I was speechless. I looked at the shimmering diamonds, then back up at my husband.

"I'd like to shower you with diamonds and so much more for putting up with me," he said. "I love you, baby."

We shared a passionate kiss that could've had us back in the bedroom instead of heading out, but I pulled back. We had plans and I wasn't about to mess up his attempt at adding a little excitement to our lives.

"Okay, enough of that, we'll get to that later," he joked. Dexter flicked his wrist and looked at his watch. I reached over and wiped my lipstick from his face, then made sure mine wasn't too smudged.

"We need to run. We can't be late," he warned.

"Late to what? Where are we going?" I asked, faking frustration.

Dexter opened the front door and led me by the arm out to a waiting car. He never answered my question.

Dexter

The night was going smoothly. I had everything planned, down to the very second. With Larry helping out at the airport, Roger was responsible for dropping my car at the hotel. That's where we'd end up once the night was over. I'd booked a room for us at the new Hilton in downtown Houston—the anniversary suite, of course.

By the time I led Keisha out to the waiting limo, I was glad to see Roger had already been by to pick up my car. I had told the limo driver to take the scenic route to our destination. After about twenty minutes of riding around downtown Houston, I'd have Keisha put the blindfold on.

Keisha sat sipping on champagne, and giving me some of the most seductive looks I had seen in a while. I really wished I could treat her like this every day.

"You better be glad we have plans tonight," she said.

"Oh, you haven't seen anything yet," I promised.

She sipped and nodded, still looking at me with sexy eyes. I wanted to rip that dress from her body and show her just how much I still loved her, but I knew we'd get to that in time.

When the driver tapped on the glass that separated us, I knew it was my cue to have her cover up.

"Okay, Keisha. I need you to put the blindfold on. We're almost there," I said.

"Where are we going, again?"

"Nice try," I winked.

Keisha pouted, drained her glass, then carefully pulled the mask over her eyes. She crossed her arms at her chest, huffed, then pouted again.

"This better be good," she warned. With Keisha now blindfolded, I gave the driver the signal and he immediately drove to our destination. When the driver pulled up in front of the building, I helped Keisha out of the limo and led her into the building and into the elevator.

"Where are we?" she quizzed. "Why won't you let me see anything?"

"Just trust your man, baby. Just trust your man," I said.

Once the elevator doors opened and the music blasted through speakers, Keisha snatched the blindfold from her face.

"Surprise!" the crowd cheered.

She turned to me, and smacked my chest. "You didn't! You did not throw me a surprise party at my most favorite place in all of Houston!" She playfully smacked my chest again. "You didn't!" she screamed as a few coworkers, close friends, and family surrounded her.

"I did, baby, I did!"

"Oh God, I just love the Sky Bar, I'm getting you later," she cried, with a smile stretching from ear to ear.

Before Keisha could focus on her revenge, that song by the old group Tony! Toni! Toné! started flowing through the speakers. I knew my wife, and I knew she loved the Sky Bar. The club was an intimate setting with tables and a dance floor very close to the stage where a band performed twice a week. There was a huge U-shaped bar in the center of the place. There were two large terraces that overlooked the city of Houston. The view was spectacular from both angles.

It was Roger's idea to have the party at the Sky Bar, but I had to execute the plan. Despite the fact that they never cared for my wife, both my boys cared about me and knew she was what made me happy.

I figured since we had that talk, this would be a sign that I heard and understood everything she said.

"It's our ann-iver-saryyy," I sang to her.

Keisha started smiling as we walked toward the small dance floor in front of the stage. I took her into my arms and we started swaying to the music.

"I can't believe you did this," she cried.

"All for you, baby," I said.

"I love you so much," she said over the music.

Then she turned around and I started dancing with her as the music pumped through the speakers.

Looking around the room as we left the dance floor, I searched for a single face that wanted to see us together as a couple. I wanted to see at least one person who had thought it might last this long. Just one.

None of them did, not a single person. Not my friends, not my family or anyone else. They all said it wouldn't last. They said she was just killing time with me, too "worldly," as my mother put it in one of her kinder, gentler moments.

Now here we were celebrating five strong years. Some couples didn't even make it half that time, but we did. And the party was just getting started. Keisha thought the party was the pinnacle of our night.

But little did she know my biggest surprise yet would come just before Scott Gertner, the R&B band leader who was also the owner of the bar, was set to take the stage.

Keisha

The minute we stepped onto the elevator I knew exactly where we were. Back in the day, April and I used to come to the Sky Bar at least twice a month.

But lately the only action I saw was on TV. Take my husband, the couch, along with the remote, and add a cold beer and he was usually in heaven. That combination left me the odd person out.

I was so happy to be out, I could barely contain myself. Oh, he did real good this year. I was kind of surprised to see so many people gathered to help us celebrate. I knew most of them never thought Dexter and I would even make it one year, much less five.

Hmm, wonder what they're thinking now. I knew my husband was a good man, but sometimes his obsession with work pushed me to the limit.

Dexter was an air-traffic controller. Stress does not begin to explain his job and what he had to endure. He'd been doing it for ten years now, so he didn't have the crazy schedule or anything. But because he's a supervisor, he's often called away for emergencies and so forth.

I noticed my bitch of a mother-in-law lingering near the terrace, but I was not going to let that hag ruin my night. I really didn't know why Dexter even invited half the people there. He had rented the club from eight to ten, then it would be open to the public. Scott Gertner and his band were coming on at 10:30, so I wanted to be feeling nice by then. Dexter didn't really drink hard liquor while we were out. But I was on my third Lemon Drop martini.

"How did you keep this a secret for so long?" I asked, looking into his eyes as we swayed to the music.

"Baby, your man has skills," he said as he turned and shook his butt.

I wanted to reach out and squeeze it, but I didn't feel like stirring up the crowd so early. Besides, I had plans for him later.

Never in a million years would I have thought him capable of something like a surprise party. Usually for my anniversary I got a gift certificate to the Root of You day spa, or a gift card to Macy's department store.

This took some planning, and I was so happy he had taken heed of my words about the state of our marriage.

I hate to admit this, but in the past when I had thought about leaving Dexter, spite always made me stay. His best friends, Larry and Roger, hated me. His mother, Hattiemae, thought I was a shameless hoochie who was beneath her son. His sister, Janet, often looked at me with disdain or disgust, depending on her mood, and his slew of cousins and other relatives just knew our marriage wouldn't last. I even heard that there was a pool; they were taking bets on how long it would last.

Whenever I became frustrated over our lackluster relationship, I couldn't bear the thought of them being right about me, so I'd roll up my sleeves and push harder at making it work. Don't get me wrong, I do love my husband, no doubt, but I never thought marriage would be this mind-numbing.

I looked around the room at the smiling faces, but I knew the smiles were not sincere. I barely even spoke with many of the people there.

There was a time when I cared less about what people thought of me. In my pre-Dexter days, insults just rolled off my back. But something in me wanted to prove all of these people wrong, especially his mother and sister.

It was music to my ears when Hattiemae, her sister, and Hattiemae's daughter, Janet, approached us near the bar.

"We're gonna go now," Hattiemae said.

They barely looked my way. I didn't care, either. Nothing could ruin my night. When Dexter's aunt leaned in to hug him, I pushed my arm up so they could see my diamonds sparkle. They tried to act like they didn't notice the bracelet, but I knew they did. Dexter's sister, Janet, flashed a fake smile at me. But I didn't even bother trying to return it. I was trying to make it to martini number four. I turned and started swaying my hips to the music as they said their good-byes.

"You be careful tonight," his mother said sternly. "Keisha," she tossed over her shoulder. I turned back to see them leaving. If I weren't mistaken, I would've sworn Janet rolled her eyes at me when the elevator doors closed. I sure didn't miss the scorning frown plastered across her face.

"You enjoying yourself?" Dexter asked when they left.

I am now. "Not as much as I will later tonight," I whispered.

He flashed me a playful smile and stopped the waitress as we walked toward our reserved table.

"She needs a refill," he told her. "Oh, and bring me a shot of Remy Martin."

The waitress smiled and sashayed to the bar.

Our table could seat six, but Dexter and I were sitting alone.

"This was such a wonderful surprise," I said.

"Oh, you think it's over?" He slapped his chest with his palms. "Don't underestimate your man, baby," he warned with a sexy smile.

"Babe, I don't know if I can handle any more tonight," I joked.

Dexter

I had Keisha right where I wanted her. Nearly two hours into our night at the Sky Bar, she probably thought I was through. It was twenty minutes before Scott Gertner and his band were scheduled to take the stage.

Roger was standing at the entrance. He looked in our direction and shrugged. I nodded and he quickly ducked back around the corner.

Keisha was enjoying the music, dancing with her back to the club's entrance. She was sucking down drink after drink and I fought the urge to tell her to slow down. But this was our night, so if she wanted to get drunk, who was I to try and stop her?

A couple of her coworkers came over to the table to congratulate us, Keisha showed off her bracelet and they talked for a little while, then her coworkers left.

I was a little upset about Mama leaving so early, but then I decided it was probably better that way. I had a feeling she, my aunt, and my sister were probably sitting in Denny's dogging Keisha out that very minute.

I had no idea why they hated her so much. I used to

pray Mama would grow close to my wife, but after a few years, I just said forget it. I kinda figured Mama was uptight because she wanted me to marry her best friend's daughter. And since I didn't, she took it as a personal betrayal.

Pauline White was not my type by a long shot. I have nothing against big girls, but she was more sloppy than she was big. It looked like she just didn't care. Pauline and I were friends all through elementary, middle, and high school, but I really only wanted her as a friend.

She's an attorney now, but all the success in the world wouldn't make me be with a woman who didn't care about what she looked like. Besides, she didn't light my fire like Keisha. I believe my mother never quite got over that, either. It was like she and Marie, Pauline's mother, had our wedding planned before we were even out of our walkers.

"Earth to Dexter, ahh, heello Dexter?" Keisha said.

"Oh, I'm sorry, my mind was somewhere else, but what's up?"

"I was just thanking you again for this. I still can't believe you planned a surprise party for our anniversary and nobody spilled the beans," Keisha said.

I shrugged, but I knew most of the people were there because of me, and probably wouldn't tell her because that would mean they'd have to actually speak to her.

When I saw Roger walk around the corner and back into the club, I was a little worried because I didn't see anyone else with him. My eyes quickly darted in his direction.

I saw him turn and reach back around the corner as if he was trying to convince someone to come into the club.

Keisha turned her head to see what was holding my attention near the entrance.

"See somebody you know?" she asked.

"No, I was trying to see what Roger was up to." I looked over Keisha's shoulder again. Then I reached over and kissed her.

"I know things haven't exactly been perfect with us, especially with me and work lately, but I'm just glad you stuck by my side and didn't give up. I know it's hard getting along with my family, and my friends are always acting standoffish, but you know how much I love you, right?"

Keisha took my hands and kissed my fingers. "I don't care what anybody thinks about me. I love you for loving me," she said. "I know they don't want us together. They think you made a mistake by marrying me. But I'm just glad that you believe people can change, and I love you for believing in me," she said.

"Hey, this is a celebration. Don't go getting all emotional on me. You know I don't care what none of these people think. You're all that matters to me, you know that, right?"

I was glad to see her smile again. The waitress came with another Lemon Drop martini. My baby got up out of her chair, shook that phat ass of hers and sat back down to take a sip. After that sip, she rushed over and flopped onto my lap. That's when I knew for sure she was nice and drunk. Keisha got up to go back to her seat and stopped cold in her tracks. She looked toward the club's entrance and her mouth dropped.

When she turned to look back at me her eyes were filled with tears. She quickly looked back toward the entrance.

"Happy anniversary, baby," I said.

Keisha

"Ohmygod!" I squealed.

I looked at Dexter, then back toward the entrance.

"This cannot be real," I screamed.

"Happy anniversary, baby," he said. My husband was the man! No doubt!

The tears that had pooled in my eyes were now running freely down my cheeks. I didn't care because they were tears of sheer joy. I could hardly believe my eyes. There was simply no way. I kept shaking my head and looking back at Dexter.

"Go," he urged, using his hands to motion me toward the front of the club.

I couldn't move. I didn't know what to say or do. "How did you find her?" I finally managed.

"Go," he insisted, again making shoving motions with both hands.

I'm not sure if it was April or me who started running first. But when we reached each other's arms, it was as if we had never been separated.

"Goodness!" she squealed. "Let me look at your fine-ass self!"

"What are you doing here?" I cried.

"Ask that wonderful husband of yours," she said.

We embraced again, rocking back and forth, holding each other tightly. I had dreamed of seeing April again, but never thought it possible. We lost contact right after my wedding.

She had flown to the Bahamas with the new man she was seeing at the time and I was so thrilled to see her come back. But I also knew back then that I probably wouldn't see her again for a very long time though I never expected five years to pass before our next visit. I guess we just got caught up in our own lives.

April had come to me before sunup the day after my wedding. She told me she and her new man were thinking about getting married. I thought it strange, since she had just met him a few days before the trip and a week after her first divorce was final. I didn't even remember his name, but for some reason they couldn't stay in the Bahamas. She said he had to report for camp. I didn't even bother asking what kind of camp. That had been five years ago. Five long years!

After another hug, I stepped back to look at her.

"What are you doing here?" I asked again.

"Girl, you've got a good one there. He paid somebody damn to find my ass," she stepped back and snapped her fingers, "and voilà! Here I am!"

I turned briefly to look back at our table. Dexter raised his glass to me. I smiled, shook my head, and turned back to April.

"How long are you in town? I can't believe you're here," I said.

"Ooouch!" She slapped my hand away. "Why'd you pinch me?"

"I just wanted to make sure this was not a dream," I said.

"Girl, you still just as silly as I remember," she squealed.

April looked good. She was sporting a short curly afro, her body was slim, and her skin looked flawless. The years had been very kind to her. As we stood there, it seemed like old times again. I noticed men falling all over themselves to steal a glance at her.

That's what I remembered most about April: she was an absolute man magnet. All she had to do was sashay into the room and all of the men would start falling all over themselves.

April leaned in closer. "I know you're gonna take care of him for this later tonight, right?" she winked.

"Girl, I was about to pull him up out of here an hour ago. Oh he's getting his, tonight, for sure," I confirmed.

"Good, 'cause you know if you don't do your job at home, there's always some skeezer out here waiting to slide in and take your place."

I knew I was a bit tipsy, but I didn't know where all of that was coming from. In the past April had never, ever been threatened by other women.

"Huh?" I knew I thought it, but didn't realize I had actually said it.

"Yeah, girl, see you been married for a minute so you're out of the loop. Sistahs nowadays ain't no joke. They are straight shiesty. How you think I lost my second husband? These women out here are beyond desperate, chile. Girl, you better hold on to your man!" she warned.

I thought it was strange that April was issuing such advice. She never used to worry about those types of things, but I just chalked it up as me not knowing the new April. After all, it had been more than a few years since we had laid eyes on each other, and even longer since we had spent any real kind of time together.

April looked around the club. "Now, let's get over there to that handsome husband of yours before some hussy tries to slide into your seat."

When we arrived at the table, I ran to Dexter's side.

"Thank you for doing this."

He shrugged. "Doing what?" he played silly. "Getting her here?"

"I can't believe you found my best friend and brought her here to our anniversary celebration. You are the best husband to ever walk the earth," I said.

We started kissing and it seemed like the entire club broke into applause.

"Okay, okay, break it up," April said.

When I turned, Roger was standing next to her. I looked at Dexter and shook my head.

It was like the old days when April and I took Dexter and Roger out to the dance floor. By then, Scott was at the mic, singing of all songs, "Brick House." Needless to say, April and I were on fire. After a while, Roger and Dexter simply walked off the dance floor. It was no surprise they couldn't hang.

Dexter

I would've paid millions of dollars for the smile that spread across Keisha's face when she finally laid eyes on April. That was my finale.

I knew it had been lonely for her here in Houston, surrounded by my family members and none of hers, especially considering how she and my family never really got along.

Keisha was from Chicago, and most of her family was still there. I had hoped my mom and sister would be the extended family and support she needed, but they just didn't hit if off. And after a while, it seemed like they had all just given up.

When Scott and his band took the stage and did a set, Keisha all but dragged me out to the dance floor. Roger was with us through "Brick House" and a few other favorites. But it didn't take long for him to give up for good. We both walked off in protest. I may have left the dance floor, but after resting a minute I was ready to tackle the challenge again. It didn't take long for some brother to step up to the plate and move in on April.

My wife seemed truly happy to have her near. Once

again April and Keisha had the floor hopping. I started to leave again, but Keisha must've sensed my uneasiness and moved her body closer to mine.

"I think I'm the luckiest woman alive," she said.

Before I could respond, she turned her back to me. I whispered in her ear.

"I'm so glad you're happy. I hope this is the best anniversary ever."

Keisha turned to face me. For a few minutes she stared deeply into my eyes. "I don't know how you found her, but I'm glad you did."

I felt good, like I had accomplished something. I knew she would be happy to finally have her best friend back in her life. That night I had no way of knowing how April's return would threaten all Keisha and I had worked so hard to maintain.

Keisha

With my head flung back and my heart about to detonate, I finally exhaled. I had to release the powerful grip I had on the sides of Dexter's head, allowing him to raise up from his knees. In one quick motion our tongues intertwined. I squeezed my eyes shut and savored the warmth and sweetness of his mouth.

I was so drunk with passion and wanted him to know I was greedily accepting everything he had to offer.

"Good for you?" he asked as steam rose from his body. I wanted it to last forever, but I knew it wouldn't. Now in his arms, I nodded first, then whispered a hot and heavy, "Yes. Sooo good. I've missed you so much."

The steam worked as an aphrodisiac as the hot water pricked our skin. I wanted more of him, but was prepared to be satisfied with what he had already given.

Dexter took the soap and began washing me, as he insisted on doing when we showered together. That's when I knew the fervor was over.

I looked over at his sleeping body and wondered how I could've ever considered leaving him. We were so good together. A couple of years back he wanted a baby, but I knew as much as he worked I'd basically be stuck caring for the child alone, so I told him I wasn't ready.

I knew his job was stressful, but I constantly reminded Dexter that home was just as important as work. Last night we made love like newlyweds, and I was happy, but more important, I was satisfied.

I still found it hard to believe that he had tracked down April and brought her back home. April was originally from Houston and swore she was gone for good when she followed her first husband away.

We had made plans to meet at our old spot the next day, so, needless to say, I couldn't wait.

When I pulled into the parking lot for "This is it" soul food restaurant, I rushed to get inside. April was in line selecting her food when I snuck up behind her.

"Hey, April," I greeted.

"Whoa chile, you nearly scared me to death!" she wailed.

We took our trays to a table near the big-screen TV and pigged out like the old days. April and I went to Texas Southern University together. But we knew each other before because shortly after her parent's divorce, her mother moved here to Houston. And even after her father was granted visitation, which meant she spent summers and holidays in Chicago, it didn't cause a disruption in our friendship. We'd been friends since middle school.

And while we've had our differences, we've never been separated longer than the time we both got married and went our separate ways. For April it was her second marriage, for me it had been and still was Dexter.

"So is your husband here with you?" I asked.

April stuffed her mouth, so I had to wait for her answer.

"Girl, I don't know what happened to my luck, but I just keep landing these fools and I'm truly tired." April sighed. She looked up from her plate. "We should all be as lucky as you to land ourselves Mr. Right."

"Yeah, Dexter is a real prize," I said.

"So what's it like to be married for five whole years?" April asked in astonishment.

"Girl, I can tell you for sure, it hasn't been easy. Marriage isn't anything but a whole lot of hard work," I confessed.

"You don't think I know. Remember, this is your first. Shoot, what, it's been five years since we've seen each other?" April stuffed her mouth, then sipped from her drink. "I've been married three times, and am about to get my third divorce!" she spat.

"What!" I asked a little more excitedly than I wanted.

I didn't know she and her second husband weren't together anymore. I didn't really know what to say. The last time I saw April, she was all lovey-dovey with her second husband. As a matter of fact, they were just getting married.

"That guy, Dan, I thought you two were still together," I said. "Isn't he the one you brought to my wedding?" I asked.

"Yes, Dan is a pro baseball player. I liked him, but the competition was far too fierce. I mean women were throwing themselves and their pussies at him like they were going out of style. I just finally threw in the towel and gave up." April sipped from her ice tea. "I met Rex Washington at the courthouse when I went to file my divorce papers against Dan."

April was in a world all her own. "I had to work that

one quick, 'cause I had the papers sent to his beach home in Malibu," she said.

"Huh?"

"Well, here's the deal," she leaned in as if someone might be listening. "I had the papers sent to that house because I knew he wouldn't be there. So they kept trying to deliver and when they finally gave up, I think after three tries, they granted me the divorce," she said easily.

"Wait, how's that possible? Are you saying a judge approved a divorce without your husband's presence?" I was truly confused.

"Yes, it was like he didn't respond. I wasn't sure if it was going to work, so I only asked for six grand a month in alimony, but once that went through, I kicked myself for not asking for more," she said.

"Wait, so let me get this straight. You mean to tell me you got a divorce without your husband agreeing?"

"That's a way to look at it." April leaned back. "I needed that little bit of a change, anyway," she said.

"So he had to pay you?" I couldn't believe it.

"Yup, well, at least until his lawyer got wind of it and tried to take me back to court. But by then I had already met Rex and I didn't really care," April shrugged.

"Rex?" I asked, unable to hide my surprise.

"Yeah, he was going to be my Dexter. He was a prosecutor, very handsome, very into me. And I was into him, too," April confessed.

"Then what's the problem? I mean, if you're into him and so forth, why aren't you guys getting along?"

"Girl, that fool was nothing like I thought he was. But that's okay, 'cause I'm about to get rid of him real soon."

"Well, what's the holdup?" I asked.

"Nothing, really, we just have to wait for our case to be called up for the show," April said easily.

That was just like April. She'd toss out some crazy shit, then move on like I was automatically supposed to know what she was talking about.

"The show?" I finally gave in. "As in a TV show show?"

"Yeah, girl, I'm going on Judge Maxine," she said straightforwardly, like that was the normal thing to do.

I nearly choked on my food. "Judge Maxine? That lady judge on TV?"

April nodded. "Yup, you know they pay you to go on there, right?"

"Wait, let me make sure I heard you correctly. You are getting a divorce from your third husband on national TV?"

"Yeah, and did I mention I get paid to do it, too?" she smiled, then stuffed her mouth.

Dexter

I thought it would be a nice surprise for Keisha to see April. My original plan was for April and Keisha to visit for a day or two, then stay in touch over the phone and e-mail or what have you.

I had no idea when April showed up that she didn't have a job to return to back at home. I also didn't know she was headed to court to divorce her third husband. It sure would have been nice if I had known all of that before I set out to find her. I blame myself for not at least asking her some questions.

But it didn't take long for Keisha to get me caught up on everything that was going on with April. And I was cool with that, I really was. Her friend was going through a bad time and she was just there for her. I understand that.

I'd been understanding about a lot of things. Like the last-minute three-day cruise she *had* to take with April because her soon-to-be ex-husband had backed out of the trip.

Since I'm not a water lover, I didn't really mind her going on a cruise without me. It gave me a chance to do some overtime. What made me mad was that she could've let her *husband* know something before it was time for them to rush to Galveston to board a cruise ship.

What if I had made plans to surprise her?

Which I hadn't, but what if I had?

But the one that really got me was when I showed up home after working fourteen long hours one day last week. Now I realize it was only nine at night, but can you imagine how I felt when I unlocked my front door and found a man walking from the guest bathroom toward the family room?

I had to look around to make sure I was in the right house. It was dark, but I knew my home.

I cleared my throat.

The stranger turned. "Hey, what's up, man?" He gave me the standard black-man handshake with a firm pat on the back. "I'm Maurice," he said.

I nodded. "Ah, I'm Dexter." That's when I noticed Maurice was wearing socks instead of shoes. My blood started boiling, and the questions started coming. Who was this fool? Why was he so at home in my house? But more important, why was he even in my house?

Just as I was about to ask him these important questions, April peeked her head around the corner. "Hey, Dexter. I wasn't expecting you so soon," she said as the man walked into the family room and sat next to her on the sofa. The lights were dimmed and soft music was playing.

I felt a little better when I saw my wife strolling down the stairs. "Hey, I didn't even hear you come in," she said.

Keisha must've noticed the look of confusion across my face, because she shuffled me into the kitchen, then whispered, "She didn't want to take a man to her mom's, so she asked if they could come have a few drinks here at our place."

My first thought was, why couldn't he take her out? But I tried to keep an open mind about it. I even sat and talked with them for a while. But when it got late, I had to escort April and her new friend out. It was like nobody cared that I had to go to work early the next morning.

It was two weeks after our huge anniversary celebration. April was still there, and things were getting worse. I came home one evening to find April and Keisha in the family room. There were stacks of papers everywhere. Some looked like financial documents, others were pages from spiral notebooks. I tried to act indifferent to the mess, but it was kind of hard to overlook. "What's going on here?" I asked, as I leaned down to kiss my wife.

"Oh, we're getting ready for April's court appearance. I told you she was accepted on that TV show, *Judge Maxine's Divorce Court*, didn't I?"

"Ah, no, I don't think you did," I said. "Divorce court, huh?"

Keisha was so engrossed in the paperwork, she barely looked up at me. I glanced toward the kitchen, which looked like it was shut down permanently. I was hoping she might take a hint, but she was up to her ears in paperwork.

April's paperwork.

"Anything to eat?" I asked, as I made my way into the kitchen, since my hunger was obviously a nonissue.

"Oh, baby, I thought we'd have take-out. That rib place you like so much," Keisha replied.

"Oh, cool. That'll work." I shut the refrigerator and prepared to head into our room for a quick shower.

"I want some of those baby back ribs, with the spicy honey sauce," April quickly chimed in.

"Yeah, honey, make sure you get me some of that sweet tea, too," Keisha said.

I frowned. Here I was, tired as all hell, and they expected me to go pick up the fucking food. I looked back at the family room and the stacks of paper everywhere. Just then the phone rang and I snatched it up. "Hello."

"Dexter, how are you?" my mother asked.

"Oh, I'm fine. Just a little hungry," I said, and looked at Keisha. "How are you?"

"Hungry? Where's that poor excuse of a wife of yours?" Mom asked.

"Oh, she's helping April with a project," I answered. I knew better than to mention the divorce TV show. My mother already didn't like Keisha, and even though she had only met her briefly at our wedding, she definitely couldn't stand April.

"Hmm, well, *your wife* should be taking care of her duties at home. Let that heathen friend of hers do her own damn project. Lord forgive me for cursing," Mom said.

"Look, Mom, what's going on? I need to go get some food before it gets too late," I said, losing what little patience I had left.

"Go get food? Boy, you better bring yourself on over here. I fried some catfish, made red beans and rice and corn bread."

"The sweet corn bread, Ma?" I felt my mouth watering already.

"Uh huh. I was just calling to see if you and Keisha wanted to come for dinner," my mother said.

Now I knew that was a lie. There was no way in the world my mama was about to invite Keisha over for dinner. In the five years we've been married, Keisha may have seen the inside of my mother's house three times. And two of those were when Mom was on vacation and needed someone to water the plants and feed the cat and I couldn't do it.

"Well, Keisha is busy, but maybe I can come and pick up a plate for her," I said, testing the waters.

"Emph," was all Mama said.

"Or, I could just go to the barbecue shack and pick up three plates," I pressed.

"Boy, if you don't come over here and get some of this home-cooked food, there's no telling when that wife of yours is gonna get her tail back in the kitchen," she hissed.

I looked over at Keisha and April in the family room. They were working feverishly, moving from stack to stack. Keisha would lift a folder, flip through it, then yell something to April.

She would mark it off on a list, then move on to another stack. It was mind-blowing to me, all that information they were going through. What could she possibly be working on that would require all of that paperwork?

"Hey, Keisha, Mama cooked and I'm about to get some food," I said.

She barely looked up when she answered. "Okay," she said.

I grabbed my keys and headed out the door to Mama's. I was hoping by the time I got back all that mess would be cleaned up, and April would either be on her way out or gone.

I made a mental note to remind myself to ask Keisha just exactly when April was going back home. Two weeks was fine, but now I needed my wife back. Keisha must've forgotten her complaints about the state of our marriage, because she never uttered another word about that discussion we had. Now that April was back in the picture, the work our marriage needed had surely taken a backseat.

Now, everything was all about April. She needed help with this, she needed help with that, and I was getting sick of it. Yeah, I worked a lot and since April had been around, I had been working a little more, but this thing was getting out of hand.

The minute I returned I planned to let Keisha know flat-out that things needed to change.

Keisha

I knew Dexter wanted some attention, but I had to help April get ready for her appearance on TV. This was going to be such a big deal. After April explained to me that we would get a free trip to LA and she would get paid, I was all about helping her win.

She had asked me to come to court with her and be a character witness. I could talk about the type of person April was, since I'd known her for most of her life.

I had heard Dexter talking to 'ole hateful Hattiemae. Just thinking about the vicious things she'd said about me made me mad. She'd been spiteful since day one. You know, when I first met her, I was open to liking her. I mean, Dexter and I were pretty serious by then. That must've been a bit more than six years ago.

He had invited us both out to dinner at this nice Italian restaurant. I wanted to make sure everything was perfect, including the way I was dressed, my hair, nails, you name it. Even though he wanted to pick me up, I offered to meet them at the restaurant, so Dexter wouldn't have to worry about making two stops. I really wanted to fix dinner for him and his mother, but I knew my limitations, so I agreed the restaurant was the best way to go. Besides, I felt a meeting in a public place would be easier on us both.

I arrived at the restaurant thirty minutes early. Dexter had told me how his mother absolutely despised black people's reputation for being late, and the last thing I wanted to do was give her a reason to despise me. He also told me how she was very particular about finger-nails. I made sure mine were short and clean.

In addition, Dexter mentioned that his mother pre-ferred to see women in skirts and dresses, not too short, of course. I couldn't remember the last dress I owned that wasn't short, so I went shopping, and bought one I thought would be appropriate.

I made sure I was early, dressed appropriately, and well groomed. Still, when Hattiemae Saintjohn laid eyes on me, she looked as if she had just bitten into an over-sized lemon that had gone bad, then sniffed the most foul and offensive scent.

She was a petite woman, less than five feet tall. Her pecan-colored skin was just as smooth as her son's. Her eyes were light brown with a slight slant. She wore glasses in a classy frame. But her tiny nose stayed turned so far up in the air, I swear I could see the membranes in my nostrils.

"Mom, this is the young lady I told you about. Her name is Keisha," Dexter said as he pulled her chair out.

"Hmm, she's not that filthy stripper you used to talk about all the time is she?" she snickered.

Dexter looked mortified. "Mom, don't start," he tried to warn in a stern whispered tone. I couldn't fathom why she had said that, but I was willing to try and over-look her rudeness.

"Miss Saintjohn, it's such a pleasure to finally meet you," I offered, even extending my hand, even though I wasn't sure she'd accept.

And she didn't. The old cow looked down at it, twisted up her face, then asked, "Did you say 'Miss' as in 'Miss'?" I wasn't quite sure what to say. I stood shaking my head in confusion. "I will have you know," she hissed, "I was happily married to Dexter's father for thirty-nine years before the good Lord called him home. I am Mis-sus Saintjohn," she corrected, over-enunciating the syllables.

I was so nervous, I thought I'd die right there. The evening progressed, without much improvement.

"So where are your folks from?" she later asked. I figured that was her attempt at trying to strike up a conversation, so I took the bait.

"Oh, ah, I was born here in Houston, but I have family in Chicago, ma'am."

"Good Lord, don't say the south side. Dexter, isn't that where those old neighbors of ours came from? Classless, all of 'em, the entire clan, what was their name again?" She balked and looked at Dexter with wide eyes.

"Ma, those people never did anything to you. They were pretty cool, you just never gave them a chance," he said matter-of-factly.

"Brooks, that's right. The Brooks clan, with those worldly teenage girls. I knew for sure they were trouble the instant I laid eyes on them."

I listened as she rambled on about the Brooks family. She talked about the mother's morals, how loose her girls had been, and everything down to the time male visitors would leave the house.

The way Hattiemae went on and on about the south

side of Chicago, you would've thought she had lived there or had even visited before, but I later found out she hadn't.

As I sat trying to mind my manners, she glanced over at me and said, "You could probably use a bra with more support. I always tell my daughter Janet it's important for women your age to take care of your bodies."

I was dumbfounded. How do you respond to a comment like that? I just glanced down at my chest and wondered how I could've possibly missed that.

"I'll bet you don't sleep with a bra, either, huh? I can tell," she continued before I could even fully comprehend the first comment, then finished me off with, "You'll be sagging before you nurse your first child."

Dexter's head snapped in her direction, "Ma, c'mon, now. Keisha doesn't need to hear all of that."

But it seemed the more Dexter protested, the more inappropriate Hattiemae's comments became.

"I keep telling my Dexter he needs to be careful out there, watch out for traps. I don't want no accidental babies popping up. My Dexter is a good man, he'd be a nice catch, but I'm holding out for somebody who's worthy," she said, peering down her nose over her frames at me with those beady eyes.

"If you don't stop, I'm gonna ask for the check and we're leaving," Dexter warned.

She cut it out for a little while, but after changing the subject a few times to something lighthearted, she started in again.

"Remember that little ghetto girl who tried to trap you a few years ago? Thought she had struck gold when she found out you were in school to be an air-traffic controller. Hmm, one look at that cockeyed baby and I knew that was no grandchild of mine," she hissed with pride.

I sat there numb. I wanted someone to come over and drop a hot plate of food all over me just so I'd have a legitimate excuse to get up and leave. As the night wore on, things got progressively worse. Despite the fact that nearly an hour into the already disastrous dinner I didn't think things could get any worse.

After our meals arrived, I looked up to see a younger, taller version of Hattiemae. I thought I was about to get some much-needed relief.

"Janet, what are you doing here?" Dexter asked, rising up from his seat. He and Janet hugged.

A baffled look quickly spread across Janet's face. She looked at her mother, then at Dexter. "Mom, you told me Dexter invited me to join you guys for dinner," she said, sounding a bit confused.

"Ah, you must've misunderstood," Hattiemae claimed, nervously tapping the sides of her mouth with the linen napkin.

"No, you told me where we were supposed to meet, and even what time. How could I misunderstand all those details?" Janet's hands flew to her hips.

If I knew then what I know now, I would've left Dexter's fine ass right there with his crazy-ass mama and sister.

"Keisha?" April called, snapping me out of still dealing with Hattiemae and Janet and their foolishness after all those years.

"Oh, girl, I'm sorry, my mind was somewhere else," I offered.

"I asked if you told Dexter about the trip to LA."

"No, not yet," I answered uneasily.

April's eyebrow crowded into one. "Well, damn, when

are you gonna tell him? I mean, we leave Thursday. That's the day after tomorrow," she said.

"I know, just let me handle Dexter. I'll be ready to go," I promised. But I was wondering just how in the world I'd explain yet another trip with April, especially when I knew he was just now barely getting over the first one.

Dexter

When I walked in from work Wednesday evening, the house was spotless and smelling like heaven. I had to work some overtime, so it was close to eight, but I had called to let Keisha know.

She was surprisingly pleasant about it and didn't even put up a fuss. I thought that meant she and April would be hanging out, but Keisha was in the kitchen when I got home.

"Is it my birthday or something?" I asked jokingly as I walked up behind her.

"Boy, don't be silly," she said, turning and putting a spoon in my mouth.

"Emmm, that's good, baby," I kissed her cheek. "What's gotten into you?" I asked.

"Nothing. Can't a woman fix a nice candlelight dinner for her loving husband?" she asked. When Keisha removed her apron, I noticed that she was wearing a little dainty outfit. I couldn't remember the last time I'd seen her dressed that way, and I knew she was up to something, but I wasn't about to complain.

Nearly thirty minutes after I arrived, I was sitting

across from my gorgeous wife. She fixed spaghetti with garlic bread and a salad. I was dead tired, but after the nice dinner, candlelight, and wine, I knew I had to drum up some energy to show my appreciation.

After dinner, Keisha had my slippers waiting in front of the big-screen TV in the family room and had even found the Astros game.

"Okay, did a doctor call to say I was dying tomorrow or something?" I joked.

She only giggled as she disappeared into our bedroom.

When she came back with the vanilla bean oil in her hands, I just knew I had died and gone to Heaven or something major was going on.

I leaned back and let my wife's magic fingers work out the knots and frustrations from my day. It had been a while since I'd gotten the star treatment in my own house. Lately, it seemed everything had been all about April and her problems.

Tonight there was no mention of April, her ex-husbands, or any of her pending problems. And I sure wasn't about to bring her up.

For the next hour, Keisha had me stretched out on a towel on the floor. I was at her mercy. She had warmed the oil and was using it to knead tight knots in my shoulder blade.

"What did I do to deserve such first-class treatment?" I asked, easing my head up ever so slightly.

"You like?" she ignored my question, and instead used that sexy voice I enjoyed to start humming in my ear.

"Umm," I managed.

Her hands were like magic. I suspect she knew she could get just about anything she wanted at that moment. And I wanted her to hurry because I was so full and relaxed, my sexual appetite was quickly waning. I was fighting the urge to surrender to sleep. I didn't want to disappoint Keisha, since she had worked so hard to show me a nice evening.

Soon, despite my struggle, I found myself drifting in and out of presleep. Keisha's hands were working me over and I felt nice and relaxed.

Just as I was about to drift back into sleep I felt Keisha's breath at my ear again. "Um, baby," she cooed.

I lifted my head slightly. "Huh?"

"Um, remember I was telling you about April's court date?"

"Um hmm."

"Well, she really needs me to go with her. You remember all the work we've been doing to get her ready for it, right?"

I didn't say a word. She allowed silence to hang in the air for a moment, kneading my back with wicked, tantalizing strokes.

"Well, um, she needs me to act as a character witness for her," Keisha explained. "You know, with me having known her most of her life, her lawyer thinks it'd be good to have me there for support."

I couldn't see her face, but suddenly I realized what I had done to deserve such a wonderful romantic evening.

"Well, if she needs you, I suppose you have to be there. Anyway, when is she going back home?" I slid in.

"Oh, um, didn't I tell you?" Keisha seemed to be squirming now.

"Tell me what, Keisha?" I tried to hide my irritation.

"April's mom is really sick, so she's gonna stay to care for her."

On that, I moved my body to let her know I was ready to get up. "Is that so?" I asked. It was like a vice grip had hugged my heart.

"Yeah, I thought I told you that," she said, fidgeting with the oil and a face towel she had nearby. Keisha looked everywhere but in my eyes.

"No, you didn't," I said sarcastically.

She shrugged. "Hmm, sorry about that, babe," she frowned as if her memory could make a lie the truth. "Well, back to the trip for her court appearance."

"Trip?" I asked.

No wonder she was in here trying to entice me with good food and romance. I knew something was going on, but never would I have thought she was buttering me up for something having to do with April. This little reunion was quickly starting to try my patience.

Keisha

When we stepped off the plane in sunny Los Angeles, the butterflies started swarming in the pit of my belly. I was so damn excited, I could barely control myself. April and I were going to be there for three whole days. We weren't returning to Houston until Sunday afternoon. I had never been to LA and I was beyond excited. The first thing I did was call to let Dexter know we'd made it safely, but I got his voice mail. I quickly left a message and starting taking in my new surroundings.

I took a picture of a sign at the airport that said "Welcome to Los Angeles." I wanted to see Michael Jackson's Neverland ranch and everything else. I wondered where Denzel Washington, Jamie Foxx, and Will Smith lived. I wanted to walk down Hollywood Boulevard and go to that famous wax museum.

I was in awe of just about everything. I took pictures of the palm trees. I marveled at the hustle and bustle down Century Boulevard, and the people who all looked like celebrities. LA was definitely the land of the pretty. Even when casual, most people looked like they were fully made up. I was surprised to learn that most of the movie and TV studios, including the one where *Judge Maxine's Divorce Court* was taped, were located in Burbank and not actually in Hollywood.

The studio or the show had arranged for a limo to pick us up at the airport. I felt so important. When we stepped out of baggage claim, a man holding a place card with April's name on it was standing there. I took a picture of him, too.

"Girl, I feel like a celebrity," I whispered to April, who behaved as if this was all part of her everyday routine.

We rode in style to our hotel in Burbank. I took a picture of the inside of the limo. It was far nicer than the one Dexter rented for our anniversary, but I would never tell him that.

April told me the taping would take place at 3:30 Friday afternoon. After that, we were going out to some popular nightspots, and Saturday we'd spend time sightseeing.

I was so happy to be there with April. I didn't even stop to think about what my husband was doing at home. I knew he was probably curled up on the couch watching ESPN.

When I called as we waited for our bags to be loaded into the limo, he was at work, as usual. We spoke briefly and hung up with promises to speak again after April and I checked into our hotel room.

While we never really made it to the hotel right away, we were staying at the Wyndham Bel Age. It was in West Hollywood, which was adjacent to Beverly Hills and about six miles outside of Burbank. Our hotel was in the heart of the entertainment district and I was pumped.

My eyes were glued to the view outside the limo. April reached over and touched my arm.

"What do you feel like getting into tonight?" she asked.

I shrugged. It's not like I'd ever been to LA before. I wanted to do whatever she wanted to do, or so I thought.

Dexter

I stayed in a foul mood the entire time Keisha was away. On Thursday when she left, I told myself, I'd hang with the boys and party like I was single again. Well, my intentions were there, but my heart wasn't in it, especially after working a double shift. I really wanted to go hang out with my boys. I had every intention of doing that. But once I got to the house, kicked off my shoes, and stretched out on the couch, I found it real hard to get up and find my cell phone.

When I did finally get up to go to the bathroom, I took a detour to the refrigerator. That pretty much did me in. I grabbed a cold beer and made my way back to the couch. I told myself I'd wait for Roger or Larry to call, even though I knew we had agreed to meet at this place off 45 near Greenspoint Mall. That was nearly three hours earlier.

I convinced myself they never expected me to show anyway, so I took off my pants and shirt and got back on the sofa.

Soon I found myself surfing the channels and wondering just what Keisha and April were doing. I tried to get their itinerary before they left, but Keisha said April hadn't selected a hotel.

"Who the hell travels and has no idea where they're going?" I had asked her, frustrated by their lack of preparation for this sudden trip.

"April requested a change in hotels. Why are you making such a big deal out of this?" she hissed at me. I know she thought I was just being nitpicky, but I wasn't feeling this trip and she knew it. That didn't prevent her from going, though.

"I'll call as soon as I know where we'll be staying," she assured me.

She had called when they landed, but I was at work and I really couldn't talk.

When we talked shortly thereafter, she promised she'd call once they got to the hotel, but, shoot, that had been hours ago and I still hadn't heard from her. Keisha was pissing me off, and April wasn't making the situation any easier.

I got up from the couch and stumbled to the pantry in search of food. I didn't find anything interesting, so I went to the drawer of menus and found a few delivery options.

I swallowed the last of my drink and sucked down my food. My cell phone had three voice mail messages; it was Larry and Roger dogging me for standing them up. I was more than pissed at Keisha for not calling like she promised. I felt like a fucking chump waiting by the phone for her to call.

When the phone rang, a pang of guilt shot through me. I felt bad for losing faith in her just because she was in a new place with April instead of me.

"Hey, baby, I was waiting for your call. When did you guys check into the hotel?" I asked.

"Don't even tell me that wife of yours is gone again!" Mama screamed.

I groaned. I don't know why I didn't look at the caller ID.

I could make out Janet in the background throwing in her two cents.

"Yes, chile' she done left him home alone again. What's that, twice in the last month alone? Hmm," Mama snarled. She had a habit of talking to other people in the background while she was supposed to be on the phone.

"Ma, I'm really not in the mood." I tried to reason with her.

"Shoot, I wouldn't be in a good mood either. As much time as you spend alone, you might as well be single."

I closed my eyes and cursed myself for even picking up the phone.

"Nah, girl, he hasn't said where she went trampling off to this time. But if you knew that tramp like I do, you know she and that loose friend of hers are running wild somewhere. While her husband is sitting home all by his lonesome, a damn shame," Mama said, then added, "Lord forgive me for cursing."

"Ma, I need to go," I lied.

"You need to go?" she asked, obviously annoyed. "Where the heck are you gonna go when your wife done up and left you? Who are you going with? See that's part of the problem, she knows you gonna be sitting right there waiting when she comes back. Janet says you need to go out and find a good woman who knows how to take care of a man," Mama reported.

Now, my sister Janet had a whole lot of nerve. She played that role for Mama, but she couldn't hang on to a man if her hands were plastered with crazy glue. She always told us the man was certifiably crazy, how she had to get out before things turned physical, but c'mon, how many times does the same woman run into the exact same kind of man? But I didn't feel like arguing with Janet or Mama.

"Ma, Keisha went to LA for a few days, she didn't run off and leave me. I would've gone with her, but you know I couldn't take the time off on such short notice," I lied. The truth was she never even asked me. Keisha and I had talked about taking a trip to LA together, but I guess April was able to make it happen faster. "Now, I need to get some rest. I have to work tomorrow."

"Well, we're about to let you go, but I just wish that wife of yours knew how good she has it. You're a good man, and she needs to act like she appreciates having you, that's all your sister and I are saying," Mama said. "We're just looking out for you, 'cause Lord knows nobody else is doing it."

"Okay Ma, I'll call and check on you guys tomorrow," I offered, hoping they'd let me off the phone.

"Why don't you come by after work? I'm fixing a peach cobbler." Mama knew she had me on that. Peach cobbler was my absolute favorite and Keisha didn't know the first thing about making one.

"Okay Mama, I'll see you then. Tell Janet 'night," I said and hung up before she could get in another jab about Keisha.

Around midnight I finally gave up on hearing from Keisha and drifted off to sleep.

Keisha

"Whew!" I huffed as I stumbled through the crowd and off the dance floor right behind April. We were wearing them out at the world-famous Roxberry Club on Sunset Boulevard in the heart of Hollywood.

We had already bumped into several celebrities and athletes. Everybody in the club looked like they were on the verge of being discovered, if they weren't already a celebrity.

"I couldn't live out here," I said, struggling to catch my breath. Beautiful people were crawling all over the place. I don't think I had ever seen so many beautiful men and women in all my years.

I slid into my chair across from April in the VIP section. She was playing goo-goo eyes with some man who looked familiar but I couldn't quite place. I wasn't sure if he was famous or paid to carry a ball, but in LA almost everybody looked like *somebody*. Either way he was dark chocolate and had a dangerously fine body.

"This is the life, huh?" April said as she seductively licked her lips at her admirer. It didn't take long for the waitress to come over with a bottle of champagne in a fancy ice bucket.

"Compliments of the gentleman in the light blue shirt," she said.

When April and I looked at him and his entourage he raised his glass and winked at her.

"Damn, I like the way they do things out here," she said as she took a full glass of bubbly from the waitress and raised it in his direction.

I liked it, too, after I sipped the expensive liquid. The way it laced my tongue and lightly tickled my throat told me the buyer was a big spender. I knew then April's mind was working.

Before the bottle was empty the stranger in blue was at our table and he and April were having sex with their clothes on. It didn't take long for me to start feeling like the third wheel.

I excused myself from the table and went to walk around the club a bit. Before I could take a few steps, someone lightly tugged at my arm.

"Hey, I saw you and your girl working it out earlier on the dance floor. I like the way you move," he said smoothly.

I did the right thing and raised my left hand. "I'm married," I offered and shrugged.

"Just the way I like it." He flashed a sexy smile.

I should've walked away right then and there, but something about his smile drew me to him like a hungry dog to raw meat.

"Is that so?" I teased.

He nodded and flashed that smile again, melting my heart in the process. He took me by the hand and led me over to a dark corner of the club. Now, as much as I used to go clubbing back in the day, I knew doggone well I didn't need to be hugged up in the corner, a dark corner at that, with a man, especially a single man, when I knew I was very married. Very married to a man I didn't call when we slipped into the hotel quick enough to change and bounce out like we used to do back in the day.

Despite all of that, there I was. He said Pretty Ricky was his name, and I couldn't help but laugh.

Only in LA, I thought. His name, as funny as it was, was all too fitting, cause he was one of the prettiest men I had ever seen, or seen in at least the last hour, 'cause the man who was feeling April up at our table was pretty number two.

I lied and told him my name was Vivian. He didn't say anything. He simply chuckled.

Pretty Ricky led me out to the dance floor when a sexy slow song came on. I knew I had no business grinding on that man like that, but I was feeling him, I mean really feeling him. After our provocative dance, Pretty Ricky put his pretty lips to my ear. I felt heat in several places when he whispered sweetly into my ear. "What happens in LA stays in LA," he said.

I couldn't help but laugh again. He was corny, but sexy as hell and he had me curious. Before I knew what was going on, I was in the backseat of Pretty Ricky's Hummer. He had lured me out there by saying his head was starting to hurt, and the music was preventing us from getting to know each other better.

Not only was I a married woman playing with fire, fine fire I might add, but I knew nothing good could come from me spending "alone time" with Pretty Ricky. And when I told April where I was going, instead of her attempting to talk me out of it, she smiled up at me and said she'd find me when she was ready to roll. She dismissed me with a glance back to her new lover.

Ricky didn't want to talk one bit. As a matter of fact, the minute he locked the doors on his Hummer, his mouth swallowed mine. It was shameless how easily I surrendered. I gave in like a target does to a bully. A good wife would've pushed him away, offended, and rushed back to the crowd.

A good wife would've never allowed him to lead me over to the dark corner in the first place. But the only thing I could think of at that moment was the fact that I had never felt a tongue so soft. The way it quickly flicked back and forth over mine made me wonder what it would feel like elsewhere. I didn't have to wait too long to find that out. I was a hot, wet mess, and I could almost hear the swooshing sound coming from the puddle between my legs.

Before I could say a word in protest, Pretty Ricky's hands had slipped between my thighs. He touched me in ways that I had only imagined. It was like his fingers were filled with bolts of electricity. When he slid his hand along my thighs, kneading and massaging my flesh, I thought for certain I had suddenly gone to Heaven. Despite the fact I knew I'd burn in hell for this forbidden trip to ecstasy, I was all too eager to take what he was giving.

When he eased into the danger zone and gently fingered my clit, I shamelessly spread my legs a little wider. I felt my clit getting harder beneath his touch. My head drifted back and I moaned my approval.

Pretty Ricky pulled my panties to one side and lowered his head. When he ran his tongue along my lips, I trembled at the sensation. It wasn't like I'd never felt it before, but it was the way he proceeded to lick, and suck my clit, that had me going off the deep end. I wanted to use my thighs to squeeze him still, do anything to make sure he wouldn't stop.

"Oh, Jesus!" he took my button between his teeth and raked over it slightly. Now that was new, and it was good.

My body shook.

"I don't want to come yet," I managed and pushed him up. We switched positions; with him now sitting, I quickly pulled down his pants, freed his Mandingo, straddled him, and lowered myself onto him, taking him into the wetness between my thighs.

We stared into each other's eyes as I rode him at a furious pace. My heartbeat quickened along with my pace, until our bodies shook and I screamed.

Dexter

I should not have been surprised when I arrived at Mama's and found Pauline sitting at the dinner table. Janet came rushing out of the kitchen like she didn't know what was going on. I chuckled under my breath and shook my head at Mama.

"Hey, Dex, you sure are looking nice these days. I haven't seen you in ages." Pauline stood up to greet me.

She had lost some weight, and surprisingly her hair was freshly done. I had never noticed fake nails on her in all the years I had known her, but that day her fingers were manicured, and her face was perfectly made up.

"You look nice, too, Pauline." I pecked her cheek and Mama beamed.

"Pauline just stopped in to say hello," Mama said, nervously.

"Yeah, she sure did," Janet added, a little too anxiously.

I knew I was defeated, so I took my place at the head of the table and watched them play out their orchestrated lie.

"How's your mom?" I asked Pauline.

"She's doing well, enjoying Phoenix," she said.

"Good."

"Food's almost done," Mama sang. She leaned back in her chair. "I was just telling Pauline how that Keisha ran off and left you again."

My forehead creased. "Ma, to let you tell it, Keisha and I are headed for divorce," I chuckled.

"You're not?" Pauline asked. She looked a bit perplexed, then turned to Janet for what seemed like answers.

"Well, it's just a matter of time, the way she's always picking up and running off without you. Ain't no telling what she's out there doing," Mama rushed to add. "A married woman galloping across the country without her husband, it's just a shame, a damn shame." She looked up at the ceiling and mouthed "Lord forgive me for cursing."

"So you guys aren't separated?" Pauline asked, pulling no punches.

"Separated?" I balked. "Not at all, we just celebrated five years a month ago. We're happily married. As a matter of fact, I told Mama to invite you to the party," I motioned toward Mama.

Pauline's eyebrows shot up and she twisted her neck and turned toward Mama and Janet. "Really?" she asked, still staring at the two of them.

"I thought I called and left a message on your machine about that," Mama said.

"Ms. Hattiemae, I never got that message," Pauline insisted. "As a matter of fact, when you called to invite me to dinner—"

"I think I smell that peach cobbler," Janet said, quickly rising from her chair and scrambling into the kitchen.

I chuckled again, because I knew what would happen next.

"I better go check on Janet in there. Dinner will be right out." Mama got up and left Pauline and me at the table.

She shook her head once we were alone. "I'm so sorry about this," she said. "Your mom and sister made it sound like your wife had left you and that you were devastated. They all but begged me to come over here. They told me you were expecting me." Pauline started crying softly. She waved her hand around. "I did all of this for nothing. You know this isn't even me," she said.

"But you look nice, Pauline. I mean, you've lost weight, not that there was anything wrong with you before, but you really do look good. I meant it when I said that. I know this isn't you, but maybe it should be," I offered.

She sniffled. "You think?"

"Yeah, and you know what, if I wasn't already spoken for, I might consider giving us a try," I lied to make her feel better. "But I love Keisha and I really want to make my marriage work. Trust me, it isn't easy, but I'm in it for the long haul, and I'm sure we'll make it through," I said.

Pauline shook her head. "You've always been a good person, Dex. I hope that wife of yours knows what she's got."

"Trust me, she does," I assured her.

Pauline got up from the table. "Well, I think under the circumstances I should probably get going," she said.

"What? You're not staying for dinner?" I really was shocked.

"Hmm, dinner? You know I don't need another thing to eat, especially all that fattening stuff I know your mama cooked up. I was just here because I thought something else was available," she smiled. "I'm gonna duck out of here before they come back. It really was good seeing you, Dex." Pauline hugged me, then slid out the back door.

I would never tell Keisha what my mom and sister did. That was just their way and I knew they meant well.

But that night I was fit to be tied, and ready to jump the next plane out to LA. I still hadn't heard from Keisha and I knew she had better be buried under concrete after a massive earthquake or something. I just kept thinking, she'd better know it had to be something real serious to keep her from calling me.

I had given up on her cell phone. Every time I called, voice mail picked up right away. I had no choice but to wait.

Later that night, when Roger and Larry called to give me a chance to make up for the other night, I still wasn't feeling it. I was tired of playing punk by the phone, but I really didn't feel like telling them I hadn't heard from my wife so I couldn't hook up with them.

"So what are you gonna do tonight?" Larry asked.

"Drink a few cold ones, watch the Astros. Why don't you and Roger come by?"

"Not gonna happen, Dex. Me and Roger found this spot last night, man. There were so many women there that they were all over us and the ones that weren't trying to pull a man were on the floor dancing by themselves."

"Really?"

"Yeah, Dex, you should have been there. What happened to you last night? I thought you were supposed to meet us?"

"I got in late from work. Once I got me something to

eat and had a brew, I was too tired to go anywhere," I told my friend, but the truth was something different.

"I hear ya. But look, you gonna hang out tonight, right?"

"I don't know Larry, I am kind of tired."

"Look Dex, you might as well have some fun while Keisha is gone. So I tell you what, it's eight-thirty now. Me and Roger will be there at nine-thirty."

"You not gonna make it easy on me, huh?"

"Yeah, I am. I'm gonna make it easy for you to have some fun tonight."

"Why can't I just meet y'all there?" I offered, knowing damn well that wouldn't fly.

"That's how you bullshitted us last night," Larry said, and I laughed. He had a point.

"Y'all don't even trust me to make it to the club on my own?"

"Sure, we trust you, Dex, but we gotta come that way anyway. So you be ready and standing on your lawn at nine-thirty sharp."

I laughed. "I'll be ready."

"Okay, Dex, don't make me and Roger come and drag you out," Larry said and hung up the phone.

I got up from my chair and slowly began to warm up to the idea of going out. I had to admit to myself that I had become sort of a homebody, and that I'd gotten too comfortable lately. But I was determined to go out and have myself a good time. I even decided I wouldn't answer if Keisha attempted to call while I was out.

It was obvious that she wasn't worried about me or what I was doing here all by myself. So why was I so concerned about her?

Because I love her, was the only answer I had. But I

didn't want to think about that now. I guess I wanted to stay mad at her for at least a minute.

When my escorts and I arrived at the club, it was just like Larry said: I had to beat off the women with a stick. I don't know what was going on, maybe I had a sign on my back that said fresh meat, because they were hounding me something fierce.

I danced a few times, with a few lovely ladies, and drank entirely too much, but I was having a good time. At one point, both Larry and Roger were dancing with women, so I was sitting at the table by myself. This woman walked up to the table. She was wearing black from head to toe and she was wearing it well. She wasn't that tall, maybe five three or four with curly hair that hung off her shoulder and pretty, big titties that she had on display. She stood there until I acknowledged her presence. "Hello," I said over the music.

She simply looked at me like I was a pork chop sandwich and then she finally said, "Is anybody sitting here?"

"Yes, there is. My friends are sitting there," I answered, thinking that she wanted to take the chairs to another table inside the crowded club.

"Do you think they'll mind if I join you?"

I wasn't expecting that, but I laughed and said, "Nah, them fools could care less."

When she smiled at me she had the prettiest smile I'd ever seen on a woman other than Keisha and her eyes seemed to dance when she said, "I'm Monique. What's your name?"

"I'm Dexter."

"Well it's nice to meet you Dexter," Monique said and signaled for a waitress. When the waitress arrived at the table, Monique turned to me. "Can I offer you a drink?"

Now, it's been a minute since I went to a club without

Keisha, so I admit I may be a little out of it, but in all my years I've never had a woman offer to buy me a drink at a club. It just don't happen. It's like an unwritten rule or something. But here this beautiful woman was offering to buy me a drink. I wondered if she planned on getting me drunk and seducing me? I knew that wasn't happening, but I accepted the offer anyway. "Thank you. I'll have a Heineken."

Monique ordered a sex on the beach and sent the waitress on her way. "I wanna tell you something," she said.

"What's that?"

"I don't usually do things like this," Monique said shyly.

"Like what?" I asked, playing dumb.

"I don't usually pick up men and buy them drinks at the club. But you looked so good sitting over here all by yourself that I had to come over and say something."

I put my hand over my mouth. "You picking me up?" I asked in mock surprise. "I don't know if my wife is gonna like this," I said to get the fact that I was married out of the way.

"Oh, you're married?"

"Yes," I said and held up my left hand so she could see my ring. "Just celebrated our five-year anniversary."

"Where is your wife now?"

I started to say *I have no idea where my wife is,* because I didn't, but she didn't need to know that. It would only encourage her. "She's in LA with a friend of hers."

"She must be a fool to leave a fine man like you by himself. I hope she realizes what she has."

"I think she does." I said the words, but my heart didn't believe it for a second.

It seemed the more I talked about Keisha the more

Monique kept talking to me. It went beyond me feeling like I still had it; after a few hours, it became downright comical. It was obvious that Monique didn't care what my marital status was, she was on a mission to get me.

Monique and I danced to a few songs and she had her sexy body pressed up against mine just about the whole time. There was a time, before I met Keisha, that me and Monique would have been outta there and on our way to get a room or whatever. To be totally honest, she was making it very hard for me to refuse her advances; very hard. Because the truth was, she was fine as hell and I wanted her.

I kept my composure when Monique whispered in my ear. "I want to feel you inside me."

What do you say to that? Part of me was screaming to grab her by the hand, take her outside, and fuck her in the parking lot. But instead I said, "You know, Monique, if I wasn't married and in love with my wife I would jump at an opportunity to get with you."

"Then don't let it stop you."

All I could think about at that moment was that I was so glad to have a woman who loved me, because I could not go back out on the dating scene again. Sistahs were determined and they were not stopping until they snagged a man.

I made it out of there with my conscience intact and my love for Keisha even stronger. On the way home Larry and Roger called me a pussywhipped punk when I told them about Monique. "Shit," Roger said as he drove. "I wish that a fine little muthafucka like that would push up on me. Y'all would be walking home."

"That's why I'm glad you one ugly muthafucka that can't get no play unless you pay for it," Larry joked, but Roger didn't see the humor.

As we drove, I thought about Keisha. I was still mad at her ass, but after being around a room full of desperate women, I guess I realized I missed my wife in spite of the anger.

At three in the morning, when there was no message on the machine from her, or any LA area codes on the caller ID box, I was furious.

Keisha

Before we went to the studio we got our hair, makeup, and nails done in some swanky spa. We even bought new clothes from Rodeo Drive. I was having such a good time, I was beside myself.

Walking up and down the quaint little streets in Beverly Hills I felt completely uninhibited. It was like I had become one of them, one of the pretty people. Everywhere you looked, the sun was shining, and people were happy and leisurely going about their day.

I started wondering if anyone ever worked in Beverly Hills. It was midmorning and the sidewalk cafés were bustling just like it was a Saturday afternoon.

When I mentioned this to April inside one of the many designer stores we'd entered, she leaned over and said, "That's how these people work, Keisha. Power lunches, brunches, I'll bet a movie deal is being brokered right across the street," she motioned toward a small café.

For the rest of our time in Beverly Hills, I kept walking and wondering if people leisurely lounging on sidewalk chairs were discussing the next box-office hit or if restaurant goers were going over possible movie scripts. It was all so very thrilling to me.

By the time our limo pulled up at the studio where *Judge Maxine's Divorce Court* was taped, I could barely keep my breathing steady.

We were ushered in, met the producers, and were placed in a green room. The room wasn't actually green, but it was full of food, drinks, and pastries. There was a huge plasma-screen TV that ran reruns of the show.

"Are you guys okay?" A cheerful white girl poked her head in the door.

April and I nodded.

"Okay, we'll need you both in makeup in five," she said.

I looked at April and she looked at me. We shrugged and helped ourselves to the food and drinks. After they plastered even more makeup on our faces, we were shuffled into the courtroom. Well, it's not a real courtroom, but it was made up to look like one.

Judge Maxine looked far smaller than she did on TV. But, make no mistake about it, she was completely Hollywood. People fiddled with her hair, clothes, and even touched up her makeup right up to airtime. She seemed really nice, not like the no-nonsense air she displayed on TV.

Things moved quickly. I couldn't help but wonder which part I'd be seeing at home as we went through the steps of having our case heard.

We did hear April and Rex's names over speakers. The voice said I was a character witness for the defendant April Perry Washington, who was filing for divorce.

"Good afternoon, Mr. and Mrs. Washington. Mrs. Washington, you are requesting a divorce on the grounds that your husband is not living up to his husbandly duties?" Judge Maxine asked.

My head snapped in April's direction. *What the hell?* That's when I remembered we hadn't really discussed in detail the reason *why* she was divorcing her third husband. I guess I had gotten so wrapped up in her interesting life it never even dawned on me to ask. Not to mention when she dangled a free trip to LA in front of me, well, let's just say my mind was on a one-way street at that point. I quickly fixed the expression on my face and reminded myself we were going to be on national TV, and I was supposed to be there for support.

"Yes, Your Honor, that's correct. I'd like to present exhibit A." April reached into the box and pulled a form from it.

She had three copies, one for Judge Maxine, one for Rex, and the other for herself. The bailiff walked over and took the paper.

"What is this?" Judge Maxine asked firmly.

"This is the agreement we signed when we entered into this marriage." April pointed a finger at Rex. "He promised he would provide the lifestyle I had grown accustomed to when we met. My ex-husband was a major league baseball player—"

Judge Maxine raised her hand. "Hold up a second." She put the form down. "Now what's going on here? You want a divorce and Mr. Washington, you are countersuing, asking that you not be held to the alimony promise you made. You claim you have proof your wife violated this agreement."

"That's correct, Your Honor," Rex beamed.

I had to give it to April she sure knew how to pick 'em, because Rex was finer than fine. He stood about six foot five, and he had olive-colored skin with dark, dreamy eyes and broad shoulders. And whether his clothes were from the studio or came from his closet, the man knew how to dress. The suit looked like it was sewn directly onto his frame.

As the case unfolded, I slowly started to feel like a big 'ole fool. I couldn't believe April had drug me down here on national TV claiming the sex wasn't what Rex promised, so she wanted out. I was a sucker for a free trip, but that fool told the judge and all of America that Rex was faster than a minuteman.

She went on to explain how he promised he could go all night. She also admitted that he asked her to get a job, of all things! I like to have died right there on the spot when those words tumbled from her lips. My eyes grew wide, and I just had to look away in case the camera was focused on me. *Support! Support!* I kept reminding myself.

Several times, as she spoke, the audience laughed or chuckled. By the time she was nearly done laying out her case I just wanted to run and hide. There was no way I wanted my face seen anywhere near this foolishness.

Before I realized it, I was squirming in my chair. I started feeling warm and desperate for her to wrap this mess up.

Judge Maxine would occasionally jot down something on a note pad and shake her head. She must've been ready to clown April, was all I could think of.

"So let me get this straight," Judge Maxine said, looking directly at April.

"You want to divorce your husband because he's not living up to his promises in the bedroom. He doesn't kiss the ground you walk on like he did when you first met. He had the nerve to ask you to work and he talked about the possibility of children in the future. Am I correct?"

"Yes, and I think he should pay alimony because he knew what I was accustomed to before he came along," April added with a straight face.

I couldn't believe she sat there and told the world how her second husband's alimony took care of her. I knew these were things we probably should've talked about before now, but I swear, I was so caught up in her free-willy style life and the lure of the trip, I obviously wasn't thinking straight.

I just kept thinking, *This isn't the April I used to know.* What happened to that independent woman who was always down for a good time? She done went and turned into a lazy gold digger while I wasn't watching. Oh, how I prayed Judge Maxine wouldn't call me up to speak.

When the judge allowed Rex to speak, I relaxed a bit in my chair. I actually released a huge sigh, thinking the spotlight was finally off us. Suffice to say, by the time he finished laying out his side of the story, I was ready to get up and walk out. I didn't give a rat's ass if we were on international television!

But it was Rex's secret weapon that threw the entire circus of a case into a tailspin.

Dexter

By Saturday afternoon I still hadn't heard from Keisha. Of course I was thinking the worst of the worst. Had she really run off and left me, like Mama said? She did complain about not being happy. Did she have this planned all along?

Maybe she went out there and found herself some handsome movie star type. I tried my best to be a good husband, just like my daddy. I knew I worked too much sometimes, most of the time, really. But that was only because I wanted Keisha to have the very best of everything.

I made sure she could use her paycheck to do whatever she needed. I took care of her, home, and all of the bills. I worked hard so that we could have a nice little nest egg in our golden years.

I couldn't understand where I went wrong, how she could've left, even after I'd vowed to try harder. I knew Mama and Janet could go a little overboard sometimes, but I always told Keisha she didn't marry them, she married me. Besides, they really didn't mean any harm.

It was driving me crazy trying to figure out why she

wasn't calling, and deep down I was burning with anger. I tried not to think about the fact that this was all my fault. I was the one who dug April's ass up wherever the hell she was. I invited her into my marriage and my life, and now she was eating away at our once-happy home like some out-of-control cancer, and I was sick of it.

When the phone rang, I immediately checked the caller ID box. I wasn't in the mood to talk with Mama. Roger or Larry either, for that matter. I'd made the mistake of telling them I hadn't heard from Keisha since she hit LA.

What did I do that for? They gave each other that sideways glance and I knew exactly what they were thinking.

"No shit?" Larry managed.

"Hmm," Roger added.

Honestly, by then I was thinking the same thing, too. I didn't want to cry like a little bitch or nothing, but I was mad. The real truth was that I was scared more than anything else.

When Roger called back to back, I figured I'd better answer before he and Larry came storming through my front door.

"Dawg? Whassup, man?" he asked the moment I said "hello."

"Nothing, nothing man, I'm just relaxing," I said, hoping they couldn't detect the depression in my voice.

"Hmm. What you doin' relaxing at the house *alone* when Keisha is gone? Man, you ain't right," he pressed.

I really wasn't in the mood for that, so when a call on the other line interrupted our call, I quickly said, "hold on." I put my hand over the receiver and considered not answering, but knew I had to because it could've been Keisha.

It wasn't.

"Dexter Julius Saintjohn! Boy, why haven't you been answering that phone? Janet and I were about to come on over there."

"No need, Mama, I'm fine. I just got a lot on my mind."

"Ooooh wee. Yes, Janet, you were right, he's over there all alone and depressed," I heard Mama say to my sister, who was rambling away in the background.

"Mama! Stop treating me like a child. I'm a grown man! Now I said I'm fine. I'm on the other line talking to Roger now about going out. Don't worry about me," I snapped.

"Look Dexter, I don't care how grown you get, you're always gonna be my baby! And I don't like the way that hussy wife of yours is carrying on. You know I love you, right?"

"Yeah Ma, I know. But let me handle things with Keisha, okay? I'll see you tomorrow in church," I said and clicked back to Roger. "You still there?"

"Yeah, man. I was about to hang up. I think that shit is rude as hell, keepin' a muthafucka on hold like that," Roger joked.

"I'll try to work on that," I said. I wanted to get him off the phone too, but my boy wasn't havin' it.

"Like I was sayin', what you doin' sittin' at home alone?"

"I don't have anything to do."

"You know what I mean. You could be out doing something—or are you just chillin' 'til later cause you gonna hook up with that Monique freak from last night? Please tell me that's it," he acted like he was begging.

"No, nothing like that. I'm just chillin'."

"What's with you, man?" Roger asked and before I

could answer he said, "You still ain't heard nothing from Keisha, have you?"

I started to lie and say yeah that was just her on the other line, but why lie? And then I thought, why not? "Yeah, that was her on the other line. I told her I was on the other line with you and she said she'd call me back."

"Yeah, okay, sure. So what you tellin' me is Keisha called you and you told her you were talkin' to me and Keisha didn't say, so? Stop lyin', dawg. Keisha ain't called and that was probably your mama on the other line. I'll bet you'll hang up on her sometimes, but not Keisha. Yo, look, Rog, let me call you back, this Keisha on the other line," Roger said, teasing me, but he had me right. I had known Roger and Larry a long time. We were like brothers.

"You're right, Roger. I haven't heard from Keisha and that was Mama on the other line," I finally fessed up, no need in fronting for him.

"What's up with Keisha not callin'?"

"How the fuck could I know?" I said louder than I needed to.

"Calm down, Dee, I ain't the one you mad at."

"Sorry," I spat out.

"Look man, I'll be honest with you, I knew it was a bad move when you came up with the idea to find April."

"Why didn't you say something?"

"I did. Remember me asking if you was sure you wanted to do this?" he paused and waited a second for a response. When I didn't say anything, he continued. "Look Dee, I know firsthand how wild April is, so they probably just out somewhere havin' a good time."

"That's all it is," I said and hoped that's all it was. I hoped she hadn't let April talk her into leaving me.

"Right, and that's all the more reason for you not to be sitting around that house all by yourself lookin' all stupid and shit. It's a beautiful summer day out today. You need to get out and do something. Sitting around there thinking about the shit just gonna make it seem worse."

"You're right. I'm gonna go get something to eat and then I'll come by and get you," I said and meant it.

"Where you goin' to eat at?"

"I don't know. I was thinking about eating at Miss Kitty's."

"I don't know what you wanna go there for, when I know your mama cooked."

"What?"

"I know you probably don't wanna hear this, but your mama and Janet are the two best cooks in Houston, and I know they over there in the kitchen throwin' down. So fuck Miss Kitty, you can eat there when Keisha get back. I say, let's go over there and eat, I'll tell Janet how cute she is, we pick up Larry, and go do something."

"Okay, but man, don't be looking at my sister like that, dawg," I joked, knowing he wouldn't let me get away with a quiet evening at home. And a part of me was glad for that, too.

"Where you wanna go?"

"I don't care where we go as long as it's not to a club, because I don't feel like dancing," I said and I definitely didn't feel like walking around with "taken" stamped across my forehead all night.

"You dressed?"

"No."

The doorbell rang.

"Well, put some clothes on and open the door."

Keisha

I couldn't help feeling like April should've stopped while she was ahead. Well, honestly, she was never ever really ahead. I knew for sure she should've just stopped, and even when she wouldn't, I should've gotten up and walked out.

Instead I stayed. And things only went downhill. I couldn't believe I was stuck in some Maury-type mess. I felt like an idiot for not checking April out better. It had been five whole years since we'd seen each other, and even longer since we really hung out. People change in a shorter amount of time.

So Rex went on about how the case was bogus.

"Your Honor, I *need* a divorce," he said. "In the short time we've been together, I've taken out two mortgages on my home. She wants a new Jag every six months and the bills for hair, nails, lipo, and every other laser treatment under the sun are killing me," he sighed. "Did I mention she doesn't even want to work? When I asked her to get a job to help pay some bills, she opened her date book and told me she couldn't find the time for a nine to five." The audience chuckled. "Your Honor, I asked her to try to do ten to two if she had to, I just needed her to help out."

"What did she say then?" the judge asked.

Rex shook his head. "She told me she wasn't made to take orders from anybody, especially on a night shift!" Rex was playing to the audience too. Occasionally he'd turn and talk to them like the audience was a jury.

He shook his head and continued, "But she steady got her hands open. The woman spends anywhere from five to ten thousand a month! She ain't nothing but a lazy-ass gold digger." He pulled his hand to his lips. "Ooops, can I say 'ass' on TV?" he questioned.

Again, the audience broke into laughter.

After listening to this case unfold, I had to give him that one.

After he went on about how she didn't live up to her end of this stupid agreement the fools created and signed when they were drunk and got married in Vegas after having known each other a whopping seventeen hours, yes, seventeen whole hours, he pulled out his so-called secret weapon.

I had so many opportunities to get up and walk out. And I thought about it, too. I wondered about all of the commercial breaks we see on TV. I think I was secretly drawn to the drama. It was almost too funny to be true. If I hadn't lived it myself, I'd have trouble believing the story.

Judge Maxine shook her head and even laughed quite a few times. I'm convinced she knew what was coming.

"Mr. Washington, you say you have evidence that your wife has rendered your contract null and void, correct?"

"Yes, Your Honor," Rex said coolly.

I should've known something was up because Rex

was suddenly standing straighter, and his chest was all poked out.

"Your Honor, we both agreed that if either of us cheated, and the other had proof, the accused would forfeit all claims."

"Is that right?" Judge Maxine asked and snickered. She threw her hand up.

"It is, Your Honor," Rex confirmed.

See, this is the point where April should've dropped her claim and tried to work something out. Instead, she stood there with her head held high like she had been the loyal and faithful wife. I knew I really didn't have room to talk, thanks to Pretty Ricky, but still.

Rex dug into his bag of tricks and pulled out four large envelopes. The bailiff gave two to the judge, then brought two over to our table.

Judge Maxine took them into her hands.

"Your Honor, please open the one marked 'A' first," he instructed.

April followed his instructions too. All of a sudden I heard this wail coming from April's lips as she dropped the pictures onto the floor. Judge Maxine gasped. She kept turning the pictures and her head as if she was closely examining each photo but was not sure which way was up.

As if that wasn't enough, the clincher came just soon after Rex told the judge to open the envelope marked with a "B."

"That was early in our marriage," Rex chided. "But this, what you'll find in envelope 'B' is from Thursday—last night—right here in LA!"

"Wwwhaatt? Hot off the presses, huh?" Judge Maxine teased. She tisked April and ripped open the envelope marked with a "B."

That's when I saw his fine face again. The same gorgeous chocolate man that sent us the champagne while we were at the Roxberry. It had all been a setup!

My face suddenly got hot. I didn't even get warm first; it just escalated from normal body temperature to overheated within seconds. I started nervously looking around the courtroom, wondering if somehow pictures of Pretty Ricky and me would suddenly appear. I mean I was here on April's behalf, why wouldn't Rex attack me, too?

I wanted to beg the judge for a recess. Couldn't we go to commercial or something? I needed out. I was so tempted to get up and walk—no run—out of that courtroom, but I knew that would probably only draw more attention to myself. And that was the very last thing I wanted.

I wanted desperately to evaporate. I wished I had superhero powers. I would've vanished into thin air and removed all traces of my presence.

But of course I couldn't do that. Forever the actress slash drama queen, Miss April had the nerve to faint! She did one of those sexy collapses you see in the movies. The kind where the damsel carefully hits the ground with a soft thud, nothing too hard. I'm sure she didn't want to hurt herself or ruin her clothes.

That's when I knew opportunity was knocking, and I wasted no time answering. Amid the confusion and chaos, I politely got up, used my knockoff Prada bag to shield my face from the camera and strolled out of that courtroom.

I had my story together, too. Once April came to or woke up, I'd explain to her that I simply went out in search of some cold water for her face.

I never had to use that lie, though, because in the

end, the judge granted the Washingtons their divorce, with no alimony, of course.

I was sure the editors had fun piecing together what had to be one of the funniest cases ever to come through *Judge Maxine's Divorce Court.*

April later told me she didn't mind all of the drama, not one bit, apparently. She looked me straight in the face from her hospital bed and used her fingers to count down.

"Let's see, we got a free first-class trip to LA. I got paid for being on the show. And who knows? I might even get discovered."

What? I thought. Was that even an option? I had no clue she had this hidden desire to jump-start her so-called acting career.

"I mean, this is LA, right? Somebody could've been watching and might want to offer me a role in their movie or commercial," she added.

What do you say to that kind of logic?

Dexter

I hadn't been to a strip joint since my bachelor party five years ago and, even then, I wasn't completely fond of going broke while window-shopping. That just wasn't my idea of fun. I think a woman is at her best fully dressed. I just don't think a woman's body should be on display like that.

But that's where my boys wanted to go and I agreed, considering they would have no part in the alternative—sitting at home and waiting for a phone call that apparently was not going to come.

This club was way different from what I remembered. Nowadays you could pay to get more than just a lap dance. I, of course, wasn't trying to indulge, but Roger and Larry were going buck wild.

By the time we left there Sunday morning, all three of our pockets were far lighter than when we arrived.

Larry's had several phone numbers and I couldn't keep my mind off why Keisha hadn't called. The fellas decided to crash at my place. Truth was, considering the fact that we had all been partying and drinking most of the night, it was a miracle we even made it as far as my place safely. Roger leaned back on the sofa. I was on the floor and Larry was in my recliner.

"So, dawg, when's Keisha coming back?" Larry asked.

Roger turned to me. "Yeah, and is she bringing April back?"

Larry and I both looked at Roger.

"What you asking about April for?" Larry asked, taking the words right out of my mouth.

"Yeah, man; you thinking about taking another run at April?" I pressed.

Roger waved us off. "It ain't like it'd be a bad idea. Shit, April look good with that weight she lost," he said.

"C'mon Dexter, don't even try to front like you haven't checked her out on the sly when Keisha wasn't lookin'. She's here all the time," Larry said.

I shook my head. "Nah, man, I'm not even like that," I lied. Of course I noticed that April had lost a lot of weight and I agreed it looked good on her, but that wasn't the point. "The point is, April isn't nothing but a man-eater, she ain't nothing nice—been married, what, three times now? She's in LA right now divorcing husband number three. I don't care how good she look, it just ain't worth it."

"I ain't tryin' to fall in love with her, I just wanna hit it, drop her off, and let the next chump get it," Roger said.

Larry held up his hand for a high five. "Tag up; I'm right behind ya, dawg," he said, and he and Roger slapped hands.

"That's my point exactly. Why would you want a woman like this?" I stretched out on the floor. "Now Keisha, that's more my speed."

I saw Larry and Roger exchange sideways glances. I know they look at April and my wife and see the same person. But I know better. Keisha is nothing like April. She's a warm, loving woman, and I know she loves me.

"Birds of a feather," Roger said.

Larry chuckled.

"Aw, man, that's a bunch of shit. Keisha's nothing like April. Far from it," I defended.

Larry stopped laughing and looked at me. "Where's Keisha at, Dee? Why she can't even call you to say, hey muthafucka, I'm alive."

Roger and Larry didn't say anything else.

I had been wondering all weekend what could prevent my loving wife from calling home. I knew she was due back the next day, but, honestly, I wasn't even sure if she was coming back. I hadn't told them about the problems that Keisha and I had been having and I wasn't gonna do it then. That would just have thrown fuel on their fire, and I didn't want to hear it. Not when I was already uncertain regarding our relationship. Her behavior since April had gotten here had me nervous. It wasn't necessarily Keisha I was worried about. I trusted my wife, but pair her with April and her saying that she was so bored lately. That was definitely a bad combination and obviously one I didn't know what to expect from.

When I heard Roger and Larry snoring, I closed my eyes but couldn't sleep. I kept thinking about Keisha and that something must have happened to them or someone must've kidnapped her and April. There was just no conceivable way she would be alive and well and not attempt to contact me. I didn't even know when her plane was supposed to come in. Usually, when she traveled, I was her ride to and from the airport.

Since April had been back, Keisha hadn't asked for a single ride. When she and April traveled, it was like one day my wife was here, the next, she was gone. When I thought about it, I realized that April represented the life she left behind before we got married. Keisha said she was tired of that lifestyle by the time we hooked up. But what if now she missed that life—the constant partying, drinking, and men?

I got up off the floor, left the fellas laid out in the family room and stumbled to my bedroom. I don't know why I even went back there. The moment I strolled into our room, I started missing Keisha even more.

Everything in our bedroom reminded me that she was gone, and the scary thing was, I had no idea if she would come back to me.

But the truth was, I had no one to blame but myself. I knew I'd become comfortable in other relationships and that had led to complacency. I realized that maybe working so much overtime the way I did had opened the door for Keisha to walk out. I should have paid her more attention. Taken her out sometimes for no reason at all. Sent her flowers at school the way I used to. And damned if I shouldn't have left April right where she was.

I prayed sleep would come the minute my head hit the pillow, but it didn't. Something better sprang up instead.

"That's it! Why didn't I think of this before? That's what I need to do to keep my wife happy at home, and April occupied."

Keisha

While I was messing around with April, we missed our flight back to Houston. So there we were, stuck at LAX trying to do standby. After not being able to make the last three flights, we were on our way to the nearest bar, and I didn't mind one bit.

April had met this pilot who insisted we join him for drinks. When he said "join him," I thought he meant at one of the regular airport bars. I should've known better.

I had to admit to myself, I was getting sick of April real fast, after our time in LA. I had to wonder how I never realized she was so clueless. Before long I looked up and we were in the President's lounge for our airline. I had no idea places like this even existed.

When that pilot slid his card into the keyhole and swung that door open, I swore we stepped into a whole 'nother world, and at the airport no less.

I followed April to the plush sofa. Before we were able to get comfortable, a waitress came and took our orders. They had warm food, but April wanted something different, of course. She ordered shrimp kabobs over wild rice, and they found it, too.

The pilot was nice-looking—an older white man graying at his temples. I lost all respect for him, though, when he placed a hand on April's bare thigh. Of course she had on an ultramini, and I do have to admit it, my girl was working it with a fierce pair of high-heeled stilettos.

"Where are you ladies headed?" the pilot asked. All the while, his eyes never left April's cleavage. She licked her lips and batted her eyelashes.

"We were headed to Houston, but we're game if you got a better plan," she cooed.

"Well," he looked around the room, "one of my buddies got a hotshot down to Aruba, coming back Tuesday morning," he said. "You been to Aruba, beautiful?"

April giggled and I rolled my eyes. Shit, I wasn't about to go to Aruba. I already had problems to answer to once I got home.

"Last time I was there I stayed at the Playa Linda Beach Resort," I heard her say.

"Hmm, what's that, a three star? Have you ever been to the Bucuti Beach Resort?" he motioned toward me. "The three of us could be there by sunset," he offered. "I promise you guys a real good time."

I should've just gotten up and walked out of there. I may have been able to find a flight back home. Instead I thought, *Hmm, a five- star hotel . . . in Aruba?* But I shook it off, since I knew April was not about to follow some stranger to some Caribbean spot. I eased back on the sofa and ordered my fourth margarita, top shelf, of course.

"What would we wear in Aruba?" I heard April ask. Forget *why* we would go.

"Oh, I'm sure we could find something for you two to wear. They do have shops there, you know."

I still hadn't spoken to my husband. Every time I thought about calling, I found a way to talk myself out of it, saying oh, it would be better if I explained what happened face-to-face.

I know it made no sense, but at the time, I figured why not just wait and reason with him face-to-face. Besides, I was supposed to be home by the end of the day, anyway.

Well, we did finally catch a plane. If I hadn't guzzled down those margaritas like they were water, I might have been able to change the course of our impending collision.

When the flight attendant's voice came over the loudspeaker, I thought for certain I was about to lose my current drink.

"Welcome to Aruba!" was all I remembered her cheerful voice singing. I grabbed the armrest and started looking around, confused. But I knew there was very little I could do at this point.

When our plane began to make its descent, I noticed a long line of pearly white sand lining a crystal clear blue shoreline. That should've alarmed me, but, in my tequila-induced haze, it didn't send up the red flag right away.

Our pilot friend was squeezed between April and myself in first class and the two had been whispering to each other from the moment we stepped aboard the plane.

I knew April and her new friend had been discussing the possibility, but just because something's possible doesn't mean it should happen. Who just meets a man in the airport, then runs off to a Caribbean island with him hours later?

April does.

For the life of me, I couldn't figure out why I allowed my married self to follow April and her new friend. Considering the pilot wasn't even trying to pick me up, I should've been on my way back to my husband. I just closed my eyes and tried to will myself back to Houston's Hobby airport.

Instead of going home, April, Mr. Pilot, and I were off to some boutique, where we tried on several outfits that the pilot charged to his American Express card. After we finished shopping, we went to check into our hotel room.

Now don't get me wrong, I'm not talking about a double, or even some cramped room with one queen-sized bed. We're talking a suite at one of the island's few five-star hotels.

Hours later, everything in me said to call home, it really did. But then the more I thought about it, in my drunken stupor I wondered, how would I explain leaving for LA for a few days and winding up in Aruba? Since I didn't have a good answer to my own question, I figured there was no point in calling. I had stopped drinking when I wrestled with the idea of calling home. But once I talked myself out of making the phone call, it was back to the bottle. Since I wasn't about to be the party pooper, I just went with the program.

Hours later, after a much-needed nap, followed by even more drinking, I opened my eyes and smiled up at the shining disco light spinning in the middle of a packed dance floor. My body was drenched in sweat.

April was working her pilot friend from the front and I was humping him from behind.

I may have been drunk when we stumbled off the plane and into the boutique, but after a steady stream of alcohol, I knew I had to be near passing out. I couldn't stop dancing if I wanted to. I was having a ball and I was holding my own in the liquor department, too!

But I knew if it weren't for the pounding music, the hot sweaty crowd, and the hollering and screaming, I would've been slumped over in a corner somewhere. Instead, April and I were the life of the party.

For a good forty minutes we had a cheering section that could rival any Texan home football game. And even though April and I had been separated for years, you couldn't tell when we were out there doing our thing on the dance floor. Men didn't stand a chance.

The party in Aruba lasted until the sun was coming up. But the real problem started once the party was over. It went like this: Man picks up, ah, correction, older white man picks up two young black chicks at airport. They dine on fine food and top-shelf liquor on man's tab. Man flies two black hoochie mamas out to Aruba, first class no less, new clothes, five-star hotel, and even more food and alcohol, then partying all night long.

In a perfect world Mr. older white man would just be generous and giving, and wanted to show his two new friends a good time. But in this warped world, by the time we all stumbled our drunken selves back to the hotel, Mr. older white man on Viagra was ready to reap the rewards of his generosity.

My first clue came while riding up the elevator to our

suite. He had his arms around both April and me, but his mouth was buried in hers.

All of a sudden, he turned his red face toward me and shoved my head toward his sloppy mouth.

Whoa! Hold up! Needless to say, my mere hesitation was apparently some kind of insult to him.

It didn't take long for Mr. nice, generous, older white man to quickly turn into Lucifer himself.

Dexter

When I woke up Sunday morning, I heard someone moving around in the kitchen. I was still half-asleep and confused, but I got excited. My heart started racing a bit, but I soon realized it was only Roger and Larry raiding the refrigerator in search of food.

"Hey dawg, you ain't got nothin' to eat up in this camp," Larry said, with his head still buried in the icebox. He had briefly turned to see me standing near the counter.

I rubbed my face and its three-day-old stubble, and looked around the kitchen.

"What y'all want? Pancakes? What about an omelet? Some fresh-squeezed orange or grapefruit juice?"

"That's what I'm talking about," Roger said, hopping down from the bar stool.

Larry looked up from the fridge. "Yeah, whassup?" he asked.

"Oh, and let's not forget the hash browns," I added, yawning.

Larry rubbed his hands together. "Okay, I can do hash browns."

"Yeah, well y'all can get all of that and anything else right down the street at I-Hop. Now beat it!" I pointed toward the door.

Roger sucked his teeth at me and Larry rolled his eyes. "You ain't even right, dawg," he said.

"We 'bout to bounce, anyway," Roger shook his head. "Ain't nothing up in here. The least your wife could've done was left some grub for you to snack on while she was gone," he mumbled.

"Don't worry about my wife. I'm sure she's on her way home now, and I don't want her to find you two chumps up in here, so move on."

"Yeah, well, we'll check you later, dawg," Roger said on their way out the door.

Shortly after they left, I headed to a nearby Mickey D's for a breakfast platter and ran a few errands. I wasn't in any rush to get back home, hoping Keisha would be there when I came back, but she wasn't. I didn't trip off it too much, but stayed home the rest of the day. It wasn't easy; it seemed like every little noise I heard within a ten-mile radius of our house had me jumping. Every time I heard a sound, I convinced myself it was Keisha at the door.

Of course it never was her, but my imagination instead. I was so pissed, it's probably best it wasn't her. I didn't know what to do or who to turn to next. I wanted my wife back home, if only to get some kind of explanation from her. I was mad that she hadn't called while she was away, but it was becoming obvious to me that our relationship didn't matter to her anymore.

The brilliant idea I had about fixing this mess I'd created with her and April couldn't work unless she came home. Even though I was mad as hell at her, there was a part of me that wanted to appeal to her to give us another try. I wasn't sure if she had given up on our marriage, but I felt like she at least owed me some kind of explanation. And if she hadn't given up on us, I needed to lay down the law about changes that needed to be made.

Keisha didn't make it home that night, and I fell off to sleep seething. I went back and forth with anger—angry at myself for bringing April back, and angry at my wife for not valuing our marriage enough to not run off behind her crazy friend.

I had been trying to suck it up for the last few days, but now things were really starting to get to me, and I wasn't about to try and keep my frustrations bottled. Still, a part of me was convinced my wife's body must've been lying on some metal slab in the Los Angeles county morgue.

When the phone rang, my hopes soared again, but the crash was swift and brutal. It was Mama, so I let the machine pick up. I wasn't in the mood for her or Janet's advice. I was mad, but still a bit sick with worry.

Convinced my wife had to be dead or near dead, I finally decided to do something about it. By nightfall I had called every hospital near Hollywood and in the greater Los Angeles area. I narrowed my search, thinking that TV show had to be taped in Hollywood or downtown Los Angeles. When I found no one registered under my wife's name in any of the hospitals I called, I finally dialed the authorities' office.

"Los Angeles County Sheriff's Department. Deputy Spacey. Is this an emergency?"

At first I wasn't sure if I was speaking to a recording or a real person. When he repeated the question, I quickly answered, "No."

"How may I help you?" he asked.

"Ah, I'd like to report my wife missing. Or, um, at least, I think she's missing, but I know she's there in LA, somewhere," I said. I knew instantly that this was a bad idea. I wondered if I sounded as stupid as I felt.

"Okay, well, why don't we start with your name, sir," the officer said.

"My name is Dexter Saintjohn. My wife is Keisha Saintjohn," I sighed. I felt like I was finally doing something that might bring her home.

"Your address?"

When I told him I lived in Houston, he asked, "Sir, is there a reason you can't file a missing person's report at your local law enforcement office there?"

I was thinking, *How the hell should I know where I needed to report my wife missing?*

"All I know is she went on a trip to LA with her girlfriend, they were supposed to be back before now and I haven't heard from her," I rattled off unintentionally.

"Sir, that doesn't sound like a missing person case to me. Laws, I'm sure, are different in Texas, but she may have extended her stay, maybe missed a flight? I suggest you try calling *her* again, then if you're still unable to contact her, you might want to call your local law enforcement office. Uh, there in Texas," he added.

After that useless call, I hung up the phone, gazed up at the ceiling and swallowed hard. I shook my head, dropped my pages of hospital numbers and stormed off to take a shower. I had already given up the fight. The shit was really starting to take its toll.

Keisha

I knew I had no business whisking off to Aruba like some young single black female. I'll admit, for that I was wrong. I also knew I had no business being away for four days now without contacting my husband. But my plans were to fully explain myself face-to-face, once I got home. The problem was, I couldn't seem to make it home.

I further understood, calling him from jail in a foreign country was probably not the best move, but I had no choice. I was, after all, in a very serious bind.

Things might've gone over smoothly if, when the operator asked the person who answered the phone if they would accept a collect call from an inmate in Oranjestad, Aruba, the answer had been yes.

I couldn't hear, but the operator told me a woman declined to accept the collect call. I knew then it was my mother-in-law. I wondered why *she* was at my house, but then decided I'd wait and try to call back later.

I was hoping she'd be gone by then. Then I started wondering just how we went from partying with a generous pilot to being tossed in jail in Aruba. It didn't take long for my mind to drift back to the moment that changed everything.

When I refused his advances in that elevator, he looked to April as if she was supposed to change my mind.

"She's married," April finally said to the pilot, Sam.

When Sam looked at her and said, "So what? So am I," my buzz was instantly gone.

The elevator arrived at our floor and a heated argument ensued. "Well, why you all over my girl, anyway?" April demanded to know.

Next thing I knew somebody said something about a ho', then all of our expenses were mentioned and how would we pay for the trip and I lost it.

"Look, I never asked you for anything!" I screamed at Sam.

"You knew what the hell was up," April spat at him.

"You girls need to learn how to party," Sam said. "When I invited you to tag along, I thought the terms were understood. Nothing's free in this world, didn't your mamas teach you that?" he smirked.

I don't remember who swung first, but soon we were involved in a three-person brawl, rolling on the floor and all. By the time security came, it looked as if April and I were attacking the well-respected, and obviously well-known, Mr. Ponson.

I'm not sure what happened to Sam, but they tossed April and my black ass in jail so quickly I didn't even have time to explain my side of the story.

While I sat there trying to think of something to do, April sat over in the corner and had the nerve to be sleeping!

"Okay honey, here's what happened. . . ." I shook my head. No, that won't do, "See, what had happened was . . ." Hell no! I was trying to figure out what I would sound like when I did finally speak to Dexter.

But no matter how I tried to organize the words, they just didn't sound right. One of the main problems was the fact that they were coming from my mouth, which was stuck behind bars in Aruba.

It disgusted me each time I glanced over and saw April sleeping peacefully. During a time when she should've been putting her head with mine to try and figure this mess out, she was snoring.

Realistically, I had to admit one thing, that this was definitely my fault. I had allowed April to lead me into a world of nonsense. Quite surely, my loving husband would understand. True, I had allowed myself to be led astray, but things were going to change once I got up out of jail.

The next time I called home, the operator again told me the call was denied. When the hell was Hattiemae going home? As I sat back on the bench, sleeping beauty finally opened her eyes.

"Hey, girl." April stretched and yawned. She looked around as if she wasn't quite sure where she was. "Sam didn't come and get us out yet?" she frowned.

I looked at her. "I didn't know that's what we were waiting for. How could you sleep while we're in jail?" I asked, thinking, *This girl is really special.*

"Keisha, we probably haven't had a good sleep in days now. I'm tired. We might as well get some rest." When she shrugged and closed her eyes again, I was more than a bit miffed.

"April! You don't get it. We're in jail!" I screamed.

Just then, one of the jail guards came to the cage we were being held in. I immediately ran toward the door. "Are we getting out?"

"Yes," the guard said as he unlocked the door.

April walked out smoothly as if she had no worries. I immediately felt bad about the way I had yelled at her.

We couldn't go back to the hotel, for obvious reasons, but our things were at the jail's administrative office. At least most of them were.

I knew I should've called my husband, but my main focus was how to get off that island and back home. Again I figured it would be best if I just explained face-to-face.

"What are we going to do?" I asked April as we gathered our things. Still, she didn't seem the least bit worried.

We signed the necessary papers, and were told the charges had been dropped. I was relieved, but still concerned about how I was going to get home.

Outside, April secured a ride for us. I wanted to go straight to the airport and was glad she felt the same way. With only the clothes on our backs and our belongings in our purses, we were on our way home.

I didn't stop to think about how we'd pay for our tickets, but April had us covered. We walked across the street to the cybercafé and she picked up the phone to call and order our tickets.

"Okay, that'll be twelve-hundred fifty-six dollars and eighty-four cents each," I heard April repeat to confirm.

My eyebrows shot up. Until April whipped out an American Express card and started rattling off Sam's information.

The travel agent must've asked for the billing address, because she pulled out his driver's license and supplied his address.

I just shook my head in disbelief. But I was happy to

finally be headed home. Our seven-hour flight would get us to Houston at ten Tuesday morning.

I only hoped my husband would still want me when I did finally return home.

Dexter

I was so glad I stayed home Tuesday. If I had gone to work, I would've missed Keisha when she finally came strolling through the front door. She would've been there when I got off, but I would've missed the moment I heard someone fumbling with the lock at the front door, and the look of sheer shock on her face when she saw me.

By the time I left our bedroom and walked to the hall-way I had to hold on to the banister to keep myself from doing something stupid. When the door swung open and Keisha strolled into the foyer, she stopped and stared at me.

I wanted to run to her, to kiss her and strangle her at the same time. I don't know what was going through her mind. I'm not sure if she even suspected the pain she had caused me while she was gone.

"I can explain," she mumbled.

I was still frozen when I heard her repeat herself. Once I knew for sure that she was safe, that she wasn't lying dead in a ditch, the anger started creeping up again. I nodded, turned, and walked back into our bedroom. Suddenly, just the sight of her made my stomach churn.

To make sure that message was clear, I slammed our bedroom door so hard pictures on the wall rattled. I stretched across our king-sized sleigh bed. Looking at her empty vanity, I couldn't fathom how she could stay away for days and not talk to me, then stroll through the damn door talking about how she could explain.

Despite my anger, there was still that part of me that was relieved she hadn't run off and left me. It had lingered at the very back of my mind. After all, it was Tuesday and the last time I had set eyes on my wife or spoke with her was last Thursday morning.

Moments later, the bedroom door slowly crept open. I didn't turn in its direction, but I knew she was in the room. I felt her watching over me.

It felt like hours had passed before she finally said something.

"Every time I thought about calling I figured it would be best if I waited," she began. "I knew you would be angry, and I know it doesn't make sense now, but it's what I kept telling myself. I just thought I could do a better job of explaining to you face-to-face," she spoke delicately, as if words might shatter me for certain.

I could hear her feet moving across the carpet. After a few steps she stopped. "I don't blame you for being mad. I would be, too," she said as I felt her sit on the bed and touch my arm. Keisha pulled her hand back quickly when I jumped from her touch.

"Where the hell have you been?" I demanded.

I wanted to hear the words "sorry," "I was a fool," "I didn't mean to make you worry." Instead she said, "I called a couple of times but I didn't catch you. You must've been working."

That comment made me turn over quickly. I looked at her. "I don't believe you." I sat upright on the bed. "You run off to play with your friend, obviously forgetting about your husband, and now you try to turn things around on me? Like I'm the one who did something wrong?"

Keisha hung her head and started picking at her nails.

"You've got some kind of nerve. I guess when you said you needed more excitement, you didn't care where it came from, huh?" She didn't answer or respond.

I hated to fight with my wife. But there was no way I was about to let her stroll back in like nothing ever even happened, then put the blame on me.

When I got up from the bed, I had no intentions of leaving the room, but the sudden urge to put distance between us became too much to ignore.

The phone rang when I opened the fridge for something to drink.

"Ma? How'd you know I was here?" I asked.

"I called your office, and they said you took today off," Mama said.

Truth was, I didn't hear a word my mother was saying. Secretly, I wondered how long it would take before Keisha would come after me. I was also trying to figure out how long would be a sufficient amount of time for her to suffer.

". . . so Janet and I were talking and there's this really nice young lady from church. Janet seems to think she's your type. I heard her father is on the board over at MD Anderson, so you know she comes from a good family."

"How exactly do we know that, Mama?" I chimed in, even though I could care less. It was like I had to take my frustration out on someone.

"Well, let's face it, dear, if her father's a physician and I heard her mother is a socialite who volunteers heavily, she's got to be better than . . ."

"Better than what, Ma? Better than Keisha? Go ahead and say it. Just because Keisha's mother was a single parent, you think she's beneath us. But look at Janet. She's almost forty, never been married and keeps running back home to you." I regretted it as soon as the words left my lips.

The truth, I realized, was I shouldn't have been talking to Mama or anyone else because it was obvious I wanted to lash out and hurt someone the way Keisha had hurt me.

"You and your sister both come from a long line of proud people on both your father's side, rest his soul, and mine. You both grew up in the church. Your father spent thirty-four years as a well-respected civil engineer and my years devoted to the nonprofits before I chose to stay home with you guys puts us in a class that is above that of that wife of yours! And then she has the nerve to not even attend the house of the Lord!" my mother spat.

"Ma, Keisha does go to church, and you know as well as I do, money, class, prestige, and even religion don't automatically mean you're better." I tried to reason.

"You have done this on purpose. You deliberately defy my wishes and bring these tramps just to get under my skin. Say what you want about your sister, but I didn't raise my daughter to settle for just any kind of man. I don't care if she's one hundred years old and single. I'd rather her alone than mixing and mingling with trash."

There was no use. I'm not even sure why I started this argument, knowing it would be impossible to win.

"My wife isn't trash. I'm tired of you and Janet talking about her. When you disrespect her, you disrespect me. I need to go, Ma," I said in a hurry and hung up. I wasn't sure what Mama wanted, but after that conversation, I really didn't care.

"Did you mean that?" I turned at the sound of Keisha's voice.

"You have no idea what I go through. Not even a clue," I said.

"I'm so sorry," Keisha said softly. This time when she reached for me I didn't move. She moved and sat on the sofa. Keisha wrung her hands and sighed. "Let me start at the beginning." She took a deep breath, paused, then exhaled.

When Keisha finished telling me what I was sure was a watered-down version of her time away from home, I just shook my head. I was more than mad, but I remembered the time I'd spent making deals with God if only he'd bring my wife home safely. I remembered vowing I'd work harder to change my ways. When she got to the pilot April picked up and the hotshot to Aruba, I couldn't take it anymore.

"I don't want to hear anymore. I'm just glad you're safe and back home. But you need to know something," I said with a stern voice. "If you ever leave like that, and don't find a way to call home, I don't care if you ever come back again." I struggled to take the anger out of my voice.

Keisha fell into my arms and I held her tightly as she sobbed softly. I simply closed my eyes and said a silent prayer. But this time, I was asking God for the strength to help me keep my end of the bargain I had made.

Keisha

I can't begin to describe the immense love I felt for Dexter when I heard him finally defending me to his mother. I had no idea what they were fighting over, but I felt proud that he would finally try to put her in her place, despite the guilt I felt for not calling when I should have.

The guilt about my trip with April hadn't subsided, but I was determined to work on it. When he ended his phone call, he turned to me. His stare was piercing and a bit cold.

"I'm so sorry. I know I was wrong, but really, it's just like I said before. Every time I thought about calling, I convinced myself it'd be best if I waited and explained in person," I stuttered.

"How could you sleep at night knowing you hadn't even talked to me?" he asked sincerely.

And he had a point. But I knew better than to answer that question. I knew the no-good I was up to and it didn't impact my sleep in any way whatsoever. That made me wonder if there was any hope for me. I didn't lose sleep because a part of all of the nonsense was a glimpse of that all-elusive life I wanted so badly. I was free, I was free, and I didn't have to worry about answering to anyone. I knew by picking up the phone, I might start thinking about the dozens of ways I had sold my soul to the devil for a good time. From the free trip to LA to Pretty Ricky to the first-class trip to Aruba.

"The weekend was just one big mistake after another," I offered. When his face didn't soften, my heart started beating faster. The more I thought about it, the more I decided I didn't want to lose Dexter.

"It just wasn't worth it. I should've stayed here. April is just a mess, she's not the person I used to know," I said, hoping something would strike a chord with him.

When his features softened a bit, I felt a sense of hope.

"Look, if you miss what you had with her, you need to let me know. I'm not gonna be going through this kind of shit all the time," he said firmly.

I moved closer to him. "Baby, I'm so very sorry. I promise you, it won't happen again. I just need to pay closer attention to my relationship with April."

Dexter shook his head. I felt like he wanted to hang on to the anger, but I was trying to make it hard, determined to make up with him.

"So what did you guys do this weekend, anyway? And where have you been all this time? I mean it's Tuesday. You left here for the weekend," he pressed.

When I took a deep breath and opened my mouth to speak, I was hoping Dexter would give me a sign that he didn't want to hear it, but he didn't. I gave him a very clean version of what happened, minus Pretty Ricky, of course.

"You know what, let's just move past this. You need to understand I don't want you running around with your single friend who probably has no respect for our relationship."

I agreed by nodding. I just wanted thoughts of the weekend to be over. After a little more of his standoffish behavior, Dexter finally opened his arms and welcomed me back home.

We spent the rest of the day in bed, loving and caressing each other. Unfortunately for me, I couldn't get thoughts of Pretty Ricky out of my mind. Unlike Dexter, he probably loved tons of women in the back of that Hummer. But I had chosen my husband. LA and its entire batch of pretty, tempting people were now a thing of my past.

As I watched Dexter's chest move up and down, I thought about how lucky I truly was. Not because I had gotten away with cheating, but because he had taken me back, very minimal questions asked.

When his eyes snapped open, I nearly jumped out of my skin.

"You okay?" he asked.

I placed my hand over my chest, and tried to calm my out-of-control heartbeat. "Yeah, I just thought you were sleeping. You scared me."

He rubbed the side of my cheek and said, "I didn't mean to. I felt you staring at me. And I liked it," Dexter chuckled. "I like knowing exactly where my wife is and I really like having her right where she belongs."

It wasn't late when the phone rang, but we were in bed for the night. Dexter had to go to work the next morning so I wasn't about to stay up too late.

When it rang I looked at him, thinking it might be Hattiemae or Janet. He looked at me, then picked up the phone.

"Hello," I heard him say. Dexter rolled his eyes and I

prepared for another "pleasant" argument with him and his mother. So, I braced myself.

But when he tapped me with the phone's antenna, I was more than just a little bit surprised.

"It's April," he passed me the phone with a sour look on his face and snickered. "She's crying."

Dexter got up from the bed and walked into the bathroom. I heard him in there when I put the phone to my ear.

"Hello?"

"Girl, I'm so glad you're home," she wept. I listened as she blew her nose. "Rex came by here while we were gone. And he told my mother everything. Now she's putting me out and I don't know what to do. I came here to help her out and she's going to do this to me over what some bama told her?" April was screaming.

"Okay, wait, slow down," I pleaded. I struggled to keep my voice down.

"I just need to come and crash at your place for a few weeks, just until I figure out my next move. I don't know what I'm gonna do," she cried.

I wanted to say so many things, but I couldn't find the words. I had questions, but I didn't quite know where to start. Like why would Rex even bother to tell her mother anything? But I didn't get a chance to ask a thing. Later when I did try to talk to her about the situation and just exactly what Rex had told her mother, she refused to answer my questions. I just figured there was no telling what had really happened with him and April.

"A cab's on the way, so I'm just gonna have them drop me off over there," April sobbed.

"Okay," I managed.

When Dexter walked out of the bathroom I had my

eyes closed and the phone at my chest. The dial tone was buzzing.

"You need to hang it up unless you're planning to talk to someone else at this hour," Dexter snickered.

"It's only eleven o'clock. You act like it's two in the morning," I snapped.

Dexter's eyebrows crowded into one long strand. "Whoa!" He put his hand up. "Did I miss something?"

I shook my head and before I could control them, tears started flowing. I'm not sure why I cried, but it was like I couldn't help myself.

When Dexter took my hand, I forced myself to stop crying. "What is it?" he asked. But I had the feeling he didn't really want to know. I noticed him glance at the digital clock on my side of the bed.

"April is having some problems with her mother. She needs to stay with us for a few days." I spit it out and hoped for the best.

Dexter didn't say anything right away. I figured he was trying to find a way to say "no."

"Her father let me stay with them for months during the summer when my mom was working two jobs. I owe her, honey," I pleaded.

He still didn't respond. I sucked in air and waited for some type of response from him. When the doorbell rang, I couldn't believe how fast time had flown. One second she's bawling on the phone, the next she's at the front door?

"I guess you didn't need my answer after all," Dexter said as he turned his back to me, fluffed his pillow, and lay back down.

Dexter

It had been two days since the invasion. And I still wasn't happy about having April in our house. In the past on Thursdays when I wasn't working late, Keisha and I would either go out to eat or order take-out.

This particular Thursday I had worked through lunch so I didn't have any overtime. By the time I arrived at the house, I was starving. No one was home and nothing was in the kitchen.

After being home a few minutes, I heard Keisha and April at the door.

"Honey, are you home?" Keisha screamed from the door. I was certain she saw my car outside, but I answered anyway.

"In the kitchen. What's for dinner?" I followed up right away.

She walked in with April in tow. They had several shopping bags and something from Chili's. I was quietly seething when it dawned on me that she and April had gone out to dinner.

"Oh, I brought you a cheese steak with fries," Keisha said, placing the bag on the counter.

"Thanks," I replied. I moved my face closer so she could peck my cheek.

"Hey, Dexter," April greeted me. I didn't like having her around, but I tried my best to remain cordial.

I nodded in her direction. She stood near the family room's entry for a second. "What time do you want to leave?" she asked Keisha.

The look on Keisha's face said she wasn't expecting April to ask that particular question in front of me. I stopped removing my soggy sandwich from the container and waited along with April for Keisha's answer. I was really pissed now.

"Um. Ah, I don't know yet. We're not trying to be too early, are we?" She seemed quite nervous.

"Not really, I guess. I was just checking because I'm about to go upstairs to take a bath and a nap. I'd like to leave by ten at the very latest," April said. Then she disappeared around the corner.

Before I could say anything, Keisha was at my side. "Oh, I told April I'd go have a drink or two with her tonight. She's really kind of down these days."

A pang of disappointment stabbed at me when I thought about how different our lives had become. In the beginning I took advantage of the fact that April kept Keisha busy so I could work extra hours. But on days when I felt like doing something and they already had plans, I couldn't help but feel a bit jealous and mad.

"Where are you guys going?" I asked. I wasn't really interested, but I felt kind of forgotten since she never told me about her plans anymore.

Keisha and I had talked on the phone maybe thirty minutes before I left work and she didn't mention going out with April.

For some strange reason, Keisha behaved as if she didn't feel like talking when I had questions to ask. She put a few things in the pantry, then asked, "How's your sandwich?"

"Kind of soggy, fries hard and cold," I said.

When she didn't respond, I looked up to see her staring at me, hands on her hips and a frown on her face.

"Dexter, I thought I was being thoughtful by bringing you some food and you sit and complain about it?" she hissed, like I had done something to piss *her* off.

I shook my head, confused by what had happened.

"What's with you?" I asked as I tossed the soggy bread to the side. "You ask me a question, I answer, and you start tripping?"

"You know what, Dexter, just say you don't want me to go out with April. You're funny. We used to sit in this house, day in, day out. You work as many hours as you can, then come home, stretch out on the couch with the remote. The minute I start going places with April, you start pouting. What's the problem?"

"Keisha, I never said a word about you going out with your friend, but since you brought it up, the truth is, you could've told me over the phone that you had plans."

"Why?" she asked.

"Why what? Why tell your husband you have plans? Hmm, I don't know, Keisha. That's the kind of thing married people do. It's called respect."

"Oh, so now I don't respect you?" she said sarcastically, serving up much attitude.

"Well, sometimes I think you forget you're married. April doesn't have a husband. She can run around as much as she wants, but things should be different for you, don't you think?"

She just sucked her teeth.

Keisha

April had been in our house for nearly two weeks and things just weren't the same.

I honestly didn't blame her for the budding tension between Dexter and me. He had been excessively whiny lately and I had quickly become tired of it and him. Not to mention, I was sexually frustrated because Dexter was holding out on the sex. Oftentimes he was too tired from work to even think about it, much less perform.

One Saturday afternoon, Dexter and I had the house to ourselves, since April was using my car to run errands. She had plans to return in the evening and later that night she and I were going clubbing.

I wanted to call a truce, but I didn't know the first step to take. I know he wasn't happy about having her around, but damn, I didn't think we had to keep squabbling like we were.

He was on the couch flipping through the channels, so I decided to take a chance. I went into our bedroom and pulled out my special drawer. I was going through the lingerie and sexy underwear in search of something I could use to seduce him.

When I heard the doorbell, I figured April had forgotten something. Hoping to avoid problems with her and Dexter, I rushed to the front door only to wish I hadn't. He beat me to it.

"Hi, honey!" Hattiemae cheered. Janet walked in behind her mother carrying a large basket.

"Why didn't you guys call?" Dexter asked as he stepped aside so they could come in.

"We were in the area and figured we'd stop by as a surprise." Hattiemae probably lied. She knew doggone well she wasn't just in our neighborhood. That would've been too close to slumming for her.

The moment they spotted me, the smiles instantly disappeared from their faces. I was mad at myself for running out of the room in the first place. It wasn't until Dexter followed them back to the family room that Janet said, "Oh, I didn't realize you were here. Your car is gone." She didn't even look at me, but I figured that was her form of a greeting.

"You guys aren't having car trouble are you?" Hattiemae asked Dexter.

"No, her friend has her car."

"What?" she shrieked. "Is she insured? I mean, isn't it enough that you have to put a roof over her head? Now you must provide transportation for her too?" Hattiemae pointed out. "This is worse than we thought, Janet."

I rolled my eyes at her.

She had the nerve to examine the sofa before sitting. "Dexter, you've really got to put your foot down. If that woman is involved in an accident, you will ultimately be held responsible. You may not have had any say so about her invading your space, but I mean where do you draw the line?"

As Janet placed the basket of food at her feet, it dawned on me that Hattiemae never spoke to me or even acknowledged my presence in my own damn house. I started to turn and go back into my bedroom until I heard the words that made me freeze.

"You need to toss them both out on their ears," I heard Hattiemae say.

I turned and looked at her, Janet, and Dexter. He didn't say anything. My blood started boiling. I walked closer to where they were.

"What did you just say?" My eyes narrowed as I zeroed in on Hattiemae, who rose from her seat. My heart was beating so fast, I thought I was about to have an attack.

"She's just speaking the truth. The way you keep running off and leaving my brother. We don't know why he puts up with your antics. Lord knows he's the best thing that's ever happened to you. You'd think you'd have enough sense to treat him better," Janet said, without stuttering.

I was dumbfounded. When Janet stepped in front of her mother, I looked at Dexter.

"Are you going to allow your mother and sister to disrespect me in my own damn house?"

"Technically, this is not your house! When you lucked up on my Dexter, you had no prior experience with homeownership. Don't think we don't know you only graduated from college three years ago," Hattiemae spat. "It's no secret you're nothing but a hood rat who lucked up on a good family," she continued her verbal assault, as if it was her right to speak to me any way she saw fit, in my house, no less.

Now I could swear my heart was about to come out of my chest. My hands flew to my hips. "What?" Again, I looked at Dexter.

At first he looked as if he was scared to speak. I couldn't believe it. I was fuming.

"Ma, stop it right now! I've warned you and Janet. Keisha is my wife. If you can't respect her, you're not welcome here anymore!" He shook as he spoke.

"What are you saying, son? You're putting dirty water over blood, son?" Hattiemae shrieked.

"This is not an ultimatum. If you want to be a part of my life, you must respect my wife. You don't have to sit and hold conversation with her, you don't even have to like her, but you must be respectful." He looked to Janet. "I'm so surprised at you."

I didn't feel the need to add much else until Hattiemae started back up again. "It's no secret that you came into this marriage with nothing but the rags on your back. I'm here to see you leave the same way. My husband and I didn't work to see someone like you reap the benefits of our hard labor." She turned to Dexter. "If you are willing to side with this woman over your family, then I guess this is my fault." Her lips quivered. "It just tells me I failed as a mother." When tears trickled down her cheek, I just rolled my eyes and prepared for the theatrics.

"Ma, don't start with the tears. We've been through this before. I simply ask that you and Janet respect Keisha. That doesn't say I'm siding with anyone. It's not even about that. I just want all of you to get along." He looked at me, as if I was the problem, then back at his mother and sister.

"Can't you guys just try to be nice to each other?" he asked.

"I've never had problems with Hattiemae or you, Janet. For whatever reason, you guys don't like me and that's fine. We don't have to like each other, but it's not right for you to come to my home and disrespect me."

"Well, I'm not one to bite my tongue," Hattiemae said and held her head high. She then glanced at her son, "And you know this about me. You also know I only have your best interest at heart." She dug into her large Gucci bag and pulled out a large manila folder.

"That's exactly why Janet and I came over this afternoon. We have found some information about this wife of yours that we thought you should know," Hattiemae snarled, then looked at me triumphantly.

My heart took a nosedive right down to the very tips of my toes.

Dexter

How did my day go so downhill? I was looking forward to a day alone with my wife. I had overheard her and April talking about how it would be nice if she could spend the day out. I also heard them making plans to go out later, but what could I say? If I had mentioned it, Keisha would've known I was eavesdropping, and I wasn't in the mood for more fighting.

After a breakfast of muffins and juice, I was relaxing on the couch when the doorbell rang. I knew Keisha was fumbling around in the room, so I got up to answer it.

Mama and Janet stood there like the welcoming committee and I wondered what could've been the reason for their trip. Mama used to say showing up at anyone's house unannounced was rude and tacky. But, like most of her rules, it only applied to other people.

I wasn't quite in the mood for company, especially when I had to play referee between them and Keisha.

Just as I thought things were about to calm down, Mama pulls this folder from her bag. Typically I would've ignored it altogether, but there was something about the wide-eyed fear on Keisha's face that piqued my interest.

"What's this about?" I asked, still thrown by the look on my wife's face.

Mama still had the folder in her hand. That's when Janet spoke up. "We love you and when you hurt, we hurt. These past few weeks have been especially difficult for Mama and me. When Keisha left you with not so much as a word about whether she was coming back, well, Mama and I decided to do some digging of our own."

"You did what?" My blood hit the boiling mark instantly, and my patience was wearing thin. "What do you mean, digging of your own?"

The more we spoke, the more intensely Keisha looked on. She had taken a step backward, and a frown creased her forehead, but she remained silent.

"Son, this was for your own good. You know I've never had a good feeling about her and something told me we should've done more to prevent this marriage from happening in the first place," Mama said.

"Yeah, we knew you were having trouble dealing with Daddy's death. We should've gotten help for you," Janet chimed in. She was referring to the fact that Keisha and I married about one year after we lost my father. But that had nothing to do with why I got married. They act like I'm some inexperienced head case in need of close supervision.

Sometimes I couldn't believe the two of them.

What struck me odd was when I looked at Keisha in bafflement. She actually looked petrified.

Mama ran her hand over the folder. "Well, son, I think what's in here will answer quite a few questions about her."

She looked at Keisha. "See, I knew that was you calling from jail in Aruba a few weeks ago. I stayed here on purpose to make sure that call never came through," Mama said.

"Jail? What are you guys talking about? No one's been to jail in Aruba," I said, hoping to shut Mama down.

"No one's been to jail in Aruba?" Mama repeated excitedly.

Panic raced through my veins as I turned and looked at my wife. Her sorrowful expression spoke volumes. I closed my eyes and shook my head. Why hadn't she said anything to me? Now, I was angry all over again.

I looked at Mama. "That Aruba thing, is that what this is all about?" I lied in an attempt to get them off their high horse and out of my house with their foolishness. I still wanted to know what happened in Aruba to have Keisha looking so scared, but whatever it was, we didn't need to hash it out in front of Mama and Janet.

"Mama, that's our private business, between me and my wife," I tried to sound convincing, swallowing back the bile of anger building up in me.

"So you knew about Aruba, then?" Janet asked.

I nodded. "Yeah, of course," I confirmed with a smirk.

"But you didn't tell us? Why?" Janet wanted to know. She frowned like she was really disappointed.

"Because it was not your business. It was private between my wife and me. We handled it," I looked at Mama, who didn't look the least bit convinced. "So if that's what you've got there in that envelope, save yourself the trouble," I said easily.

She glared triumphantly at Keisha. "I wish it were that simple, son. But see, I don't believe you knew a thing about your wife being jailed in Aruba. You're my child and I know you. And, I know you damn sure don't know about what's in here." She patted the envelope. "Lord forgive me for cursing."

Janet had regained her composure. It probably never dawned on her that I was lying about Aruba until Mama mentioned it.

"I'll bet that wife of yours didn't tell you about the child she gave birth to in an alley in Chicago and left for dead. Poor thing probably would've died if her mama didn't step up to the plate. This just goes to prove she's not one of us," Mama said as she turned and looked at Keisha. "Now what do you have to say for yourself. I've got it all here in black and white!" Mama screamed.

Keisha's eyes grew narrow.

Before she could respond, I snatched the folder from Mama. "What? Did you do a background check on my wife?"

"No! We hired a private investigator. Something just wasn't right about that jail incident in Aruba. I didn't go looking for this mess. It was just out there in the open!" Mama screamed.

"I want you and Janet to leave right now," I screamed. I was so mad I was shaking.

"W-what? You are putting *us* out?" Mama looked at Keisha and then Janet. "Can you believe this?" she hissed.

Janet started to gather their things.

"After what we've uncovered, you're asking us to leave?" Mama continued as they made their way to the door. "Son, you are making a huge mistake," she said as I ushered them out of my front door and locked it behind them. I needed them out of my house so that I could turn my attention to my wife. The woman I thought I knew.

Keisha

I could see the rage burning in his eyes before he even made it completely back into the family room. I felt fear creeping up in me with a vengeance.

"Who are you?" he snapped coldly, sending chills up and down my spine. Dexter shook the folder in one hand.

"I can explain."

"Before you begin with this 'explanation,' I just need to know, were you in jail in Aruba? Because you didn't say a damn thing about that when you gave me the watered-down version of where you'd been," he said, his voice laced with sarcasm.

"Um . . . I did."

"You did what?"

"I did try to tell you. . . ."

"Then how the fuck did the words not make it out of your mouth, since you tried so hard?" I flinched when he made an unexpected move.

"I can explain all of that if you'd just give me a minute," I said and tears rolled down my cheeks.

"How could you embarrass me like that? I've been

nothing but good to you!" he screamed with both fists balled. For the first time in all of our years together, I was afraid of Dexter.

"How could you have done something like that. What else is there that I don't know about you? Then to have had a baby?"

"I wish you'd let me just tell you what happened." Fresh tears pooled in my eyes.

Dexter looked at me, gnawed his lower lip, then did something I had only witnessed from his mother and sister. He turned his nose up in disgust and stormed out of the room. "Don't even bother," he said drily.

The look on his face alone was enough to make me feel like I was unworthy. A tear slid down my cheek. I had no idea why Hattiemae and her daughter hated me so much.

Minutes later, Dexter emerged from our bedroom with a packed bag. He never even glanced in my direction as he rushed to the front door.

When it slammed behind him I felt sick.

I ran to the door, but I didn't open it.

I listened intently for any sound outside the door. I just knew he'd come to his senses and come back inside so we could talk this thing through. Even when I heard his car engine kick to life, I still didn't believe he was leaving.

How could *he* leave *me*?

This wasn't how it was supposed to go.

I had spent months fighting the urge to walk out during our most trying times, but still I stayed. How could Dexter just pack a bag and run out on me like that? I wandered back to the family room, collapsed onto the sofa and started bawling.

I couldn't believe what had just happened. My

mother and sister-in-law came to my house to embarrass me and my husband had left me. "This can't be happening," I said and picked up the phone. "He has got to come back so we can talk about this," I said as I frantically dialed his cell phone.

I could explain the thing in Aruba, and I had no idea what this baby madness was all about, so that didn't really faze me. Honestly, I know this is wrong, but when I saw that envelope, I had instant flashbacks of being on Judge Maxine's and Rex pulling out the pictures of April and that dude at the club. I just knew my hateful in-laws had somehow found out about Pretty Ricky.

"Come on, baby. Answer the phone." Tears streamed down my cheeks when his voice mail picked up. I hung up and called again, and again, until Dexter turned off his phone and my calls went straight to voice mail. All I could do was think about how much I truly hated my in-laws. I hated them because they hated me for absolutely no reason whatsoever.

"Please, Dexter, come home. We need to talk about this, baby. This is not how we solve our problems," I sobbed. "Please call me back. I can explain everything if you just give me a chance. I love you."

I hung up the phone and lay down on the couch.

Pounding on the door jarred me from my sleep. I jumped up and looked around the empty house. That's when it all started coming back to me. Groggily, I went to the door and found a hysterical April. I sighed and rolled my eyes. More damn drama, just what I needed.

"Ohmygod! Have you been crying?" she asked.

"Um, yeah, but I'm fine. What's going on with you?" I quickly changed the subject.

"Girl!" She stepped inside the house. "Your car was stolen! I didn't know what to do. When I came out of the mall, at first I thought I didn't remember where I had parked, but soon I realized the damn car was gone!"

I felt like I was about to have an emotional breakdown. I could care less about the car. That could be replaced. But what would I do without Dexter? Before I could control myself, the tears started flowing again. He wasn't even fucking talking to me, and I had to call him up to explain now what happened to the damn car? I just couldn't take any more.

"Oh, shoot, girl, now don't you start crying all over again. We need to call the cops," April huffed. She led me back into the family room. I noticed she was looking around.

"Where's Dexter?" she finally asked.

"He left me," I sobbed.

April looked perplexed for a few minutes, then said, "He did what?"

"Hattiemae and Janet came over here with a folder about us being locked up and some craziness about me having a baby and abandoning it when I was younger."

"You did what? A baby?" April hollered. She sat for a moment, then blurted out, "You didn't have any babies when we were young. Where'd that come from?"

I shrugged. "I have no idea. I tried to explain to Dexter what happened in Aruba, but he stormed out, saying he didn't want to hear it. He even had a bag packed and everything."

"So why didn't you just tell him you ain't had no damn kids, none aborted, abandoned, or adopted?" she asked.

"I never got the chance. It was like they were ganging up on me, and I guess I was scared," I admitted.

April looked confused.

"When I saw that envelope she and Janet had, all I could think about was what happened in LA."

"Okay, I'll give you LA, but still, you're sitting here crying even though you know you've done nothing wrong." April shrugged. "As far as a baby's concerned, I mean. Boy, have you changed," she said. Now, that statement really left me dumbfounded.

At that, I stopped crying and looked at her. "I remember back in the day, you didn't give a damn what someone thought or said about you. I guess marriage has a way of changing that about people. Hmm, I wouldn't know because the second someone pisses me off, I'm out. I can be miserable all by my damn self."

I looked at April, who, for the first time in a long while was actually making some sense. I may have been wrong about the Aruba trip, but I didn't have a baby and I sure didn't abandon one anywhere. If Dexter didn't know me well enough to know that's not something I would do, then maybe it was best he left. "You have a good point, April," I said, sniffling.

"You damn right I do." She looked at me. "What are we going to do about the car?"

"I suppose we should call the police," I said, but I kept thinking about the many different ways I should've handled the situation with Hattiemae and Dexter.

April nodded. "Yeah, I'm so sorry, girl."

Soon, April hissed, "You don't seem the least bit worried about what happened with the car. I mean, I don't want to give Dexter something else to be mad about," she offered.

If she only knew, I thought. My mind was on Dexter and what to do about our marriage, but, since there was nothing I could do about that now, I turned to April.

"Before we call, let's walk through this again. You

pulled up to the mall—which mall?" I said with as much interest as I could muster.

"Sharpstown," April said. "Wait, no, I think it was Memorial City. Yeah, Memorial City. I went to Sharpstown first," she remembered.

"Okay, the parking lot, was it packed? Which side did you park on? Which store did you enter?"

"Well, I didn't really park in the parking lot. It was so crowded, there weren't any spaces in walking distance, so I pulled up near the back at a security entrance."

"The one in the back?" I asked.

"Yeah, by that little office over to the right. I figured that's where the workers parked. Then I came outside and the car was gone."

I thought about having to call Dexter to tell him about the car, and really didn't want to. I figured I'd think of a plan, some way out of this mess without involving my husband, who had just abandoned me.

A few hours later, we realized my car was towed and not stolen at all. After a $238 bill, April and I went to pick up the car. It may have been a minor thing, but I was glad I was able to take care of it, without turning to my husband. I had no idea how long I'd be on my own.

"So, he let them flip out on you like that?" she asked, as we drove back in the car.

"I'm just tired of them. But honestly, I'm getting tired of him, too," I said.

"Oh? What's going on?" April asked.

"Our marriage has turned routine. You know, same 'ole same 'ole. Dexter comes home from work, eats, grabs a beer, stretches out on the couch, and flips through the channels. I've stopped expecting anything different, but it does bother me that he can't take his wife out to dinner. Some nights I leave him sleeping there on that couch and go to bed alone. This wasn't the kind of marriage I envisioned," I admitted.

"So basically, he's a homebody?" April asked.

"Yes! Girl, yes! Can you imagine me with somebody who doesn't like to do a thing?" I asked, feeling as if someone finally understood my plight.

"Hmmm, wow. Every man I've married was too busy running the streets to sit on the couch for any amount of time," she said longingly.

"Yeah, but didn't you get tired of—"

"What I got tired of was my man constantly running the streets. I wanted my husband to stay at home sometime. Shit, I wouldn't care what he was doing as long as he had his ass at home. But they all wanted to chase skirts, or skirts were chasing them. Either way, I didn't get married to be alone," April spat.

I glanced over at her and wondered why she cut me off.

"Then there's the sex. Most husbands would love a woman who wanted more sex. Dexter is the opposite. The sex is just plain and ordinary." I scrunched up my nose.

"Yeah, well, try feeling like a sex machine. What about when that's all he wants to do? You spend more time in the streets than at home, but you expect to be all up in me when you are at home? I don't think so," April snapped.

I felt like telling April this was not a competition, but it soon dawned on me that she wanted a husband like the very one I had grown weary of.

Dexter

When I thought about the early years with Keisha, I couldn't help but wonder what went wrong. She had no idea how bad I wished I could just go back to those days. But no matter how much I wanted the past, things she did reminded me we were well beyond those days.

When Mama pulled out that stuff I should've known about, I just couldn't take it anymore. Our marriage might no longer be exciting to her, but she still had to respect the fact that we were married.

I believed Keisha loved me. When she wanted to, she knew just how to make me feel good. The back rubs, dinner on the table after work, slippers at the couch with the remote, yeah, she knew how to make me happy.

But lately those things were of no significance to her. It was like since April had come into our lives, my happiness had quickly taken the backseat.

"You and April going out again?" I'd ask.

"Oh, yeah, she's feeling down. She needs a pick-me-upper," Keisha would say.

And I'd fall for it. Why wouldn't I? I didn't feel threatened by Keisha going out, at first. I really believed we were committed to each other. And truthfully, I was able to work guilt-free. It didn't take long for me to realize she was no longer complaining about my extended work hours. Sometimes after hours of overtime, I'd walk in to find an empty house and no food on the table. The more I thought about it, I realized, I was probably busy trying to convince myself that I believed in our marriage, but since that conversation we had, I'd been a nervous wreck. I couldn't stop thinking that every little move she made was a prerequisite to her leaving.

"Where've you been?" I'd ask when she'd come crawling in during the wee hours of the morning.

"April and I stopped for food before coming home," she'd say.

"A married woman has no business out in the streets after two in the morning," I'd say.

Her comeback: "That must be a woman whose marriage is lacking trust."

Keisha had an answer for everything and they were all lies. Lies designed to make a fool of me. She was beginning to spend more time away from home, away from us, and it wasn't bothering her. It seemed to me like she wanted to be single again.

Well, if that was what she wanted, then fine!

When Mama mentioned Aruba, I felt like a fool. I knew she was in Aruba that weekend, but she made it sound like a complete mistake, like they'd accidentally boarded the wrong plane and wound up having to make the best of the situation.

She didn't say shit about being in jail there. Hell yeah, it bothered me, but I wasn't about to let Mama know she had completely blindsided me with that shit.

Then the whole baby thing was even more fucked up.

A few years back I had thought starting a family might make our marriage stronger. Keisha was adamant that she wasn't ready, but would be in a couple of years. That time, of course, never came. Then to hear about the baby in the alley, even if it was before my time—I just couldn't deal with that. What kind of woman would do some shit like that?

We didn't really discuss when we'd start a family, but Keisha understood that I wanted children. What kind of woman carries a child for nine months only to dump it in an alley and leave it for dead? Certainly not the kind of woman I would want to be with.

After driving around for a couple of hours it dawned on me that my plan could've used more thought. I had nowhere to go, and I wasn't about to go to Mama's. That would've only proven her right.

I stopped at a restaurant and had dinner alone. Once I finished that, I thought about going to see a movie, but didn't really feel like it.

How I wound up on Roger's doorstep was a mystery to me. When he opened the door, looked at my bag and me, he didn't say a word, just stepped aside and allowed me to come in.

"You can have the couch for as long as you need, dawg," he said as I followed him into his bachelor's pad.

When I looked around at the candles, the body oils sitting on the coffee table, and the array of CDs near his entertainment center on the floor, I suddenly felt like I was intruding.

A few seconds later, the bathroom door opened and a gorgeous woman strolled out.

"Oh, we have company," she smiled awkwardly.

That's when I saw the wineglasses, which I hadn't noticed before.

"Yeah, this is my boy Dexter, he's crashing here for a few days," Roger said.

The woman stood at the door and looked between Roger and me. She didn't say anything at first.

"Well, um, maybe I need to run out for a few," I offered, suddenly feeling very unwanted.

Roger shook his head. "Nah, don't worry about it, we were just killing time until the movie. We were going out, right Brandi?"

"Yeah, that's right. We were on our way out anyway," she said, shaking her head.

If I wasn't so mad at Keisha, I would've gone home. The way Roger and his date grabbed their things and scrambled up out of the apartment really made me feel bad.

But after they were gone, I grabbed something to drink from his refrigerator, glad he had a twelve-pack, and eased onto his sofa. I didn't quite understand how my life had become such a mess. There I was on a Saturday night at nine-thirty and I was about to call it a night. I figured that was exactly the type of stuff Keisha was complaining about with our marriage. But what could I do?

Keisha

I had no business going out on the very night my husband left me, but the alternative looked dismal. Spending a Saturday night alone with fresh memories of our most recent fight would've been downright depressing.

Once we got the car back, April looked at me and said, "I hope this didn't mess up our plans."

I simply shook my head, confirming that it hadn't.

"Good, because I have a feeling, I just know tonight's my night. There's a perfect man out there waiting for me and he ain't gonna find me if I'm at home," she said with so much conviction I wanted to believe for her.

April was not shy about letting anyone who'd listen know, she was looking for husband number four. She felt like she should keep trying until she got it right.

We were going to this club called Hush in Southwest Houston. Radio commercials were going on and on about the celebrity guest list and how women could get in free if they arrived before eleven PM.

There was this new black dress I wanted to wear, but then I wondered if that was a wise decision. The type of clothes I was buying now was more like things I'd wear back in my clubbing days.

When I left that life behind, my criteria had changed. In the dressing room I'd ask myself if this was something I'd feel comfortable wearing around Dexter. If the answer was no, I knew it needed to stay on the rack.

Since April had been back, I had made quite a few of those purchases that I knew for certain wouldn't pass the test. But shopping with April made those purchases seem just fine, especially compared to the stuff she'd buy.

Back at the house, April went upstairs to shower and change and I walked into my bedroom. I still couldn't believe that Dexter had walked out on me. The chances had been more in favor of me leaving him.

I put the TV on satellite radio and turned it up on the surround sound system. Occasionally when a good song came on, April would come to the top of the second floor landing and scream, "Keisha, girl! I know you remember this." She'd sing along, then snap her fingers and break out into a few of our infamous dance moves. I had to admit, it was just like the old days.

But the minute we'd return to getting ready, I started thinking about the good times with Dexter. Things may have gotten a bit boring, but we had had some good times. I knew I wasn't ready to give up just yet.

When I caught myself wondering where he was and what he was doing, I'd shove the thoughts out of my mind and look forward to my night out with April.

We got dressed, still jamming to the music, and having a good time, just like we used to do. Before we left, we met in the kitchen for the traditional toast and drink to a good night.

I slid behind the wheel, as April adjusted herself in the passenger's seat.

"Let's do this," she turned to me and said.

The club was nice, but the more I looked around, the lonelier I felt. I was alone most of our time there. Every so often April would emerge from the dark corner she was hugged up in.

I wasn't mad at her because she had made it quite clear why she was going out. I was more upset with myself for tagging along.

The music was good, just the way I liked it—updated, loud, and continuous. But I just wasn't feeling it. I had danced with quite a few people, but I wasn't really in rare form. I found a seat at a table near the dance floor. As I sat, a waitress came over with a drink for me.

"I didn't order this," I said.

"Your friend sent it over. She said it might help." The waitress shrugged and placed the drink on a napkin in front of me.

I had no idea where April was sitting, but she had gotten some man to buy me a drink and I was cool with that. The problem with Hypnotiq and me was the more I drank, the more I wanted.

By the time I guzzled down drink number four, one and two had started catching up with me. So much so, that when I tried to get up, I stumbled and nearly fell.

"Whoa!" a deep voice said. Strong arms reached out and broke my fall.

"Gee, thanks," I said, more than a little embarrassed.

"Hey, you okay?" He was tall, thin, light-skinned, and very handsome. He was wearing a navy suit with tie and matching silk hankie. "I'm Melvin," he said, inviting himself to join me. "You having a good time here tonight?"

"Yeah, maybe too much of a good time," I replied.

Melvin seemed nice enough, but I wasn't looking to

start a deep get-to-know-you-better conversation in the club. So before he could start with the questions, I said, "C'mon, let's go dance."

I hopped off the high chair and strutted out to the dance floor. I'm not sure if Melvin was scared or what, but when I turned around, he was still sitting at the table looking at me longingly.

The music started feeling good, and I went with the feeling. I was convinced Hypnotiq number three and four had finally kicked in. The new 50 Cent song was on and it was my jam.

I closed my eyes and let myself go. When I opened them, Melvin was invading my space on the already-packed dance floor. And the brotha could move, too.

Never one to back down from a dance challenge, I started turning it up a bit. Soon, he and I were going at it like our lives depended on us cutting it up out there.

Four songs later, he leaned in and huffed, "You want a drink? I could use another one."

Before I could answer, he had taken me by the hand and led me off the floor. Our table was still empty, considering how the DJ was doing his thing.

When the waitress came over, he ordered himself a Grey Goose on the rocks and asked what I was having. "I need water."

He tossed me a sideways glance, then sent the waitress on her way.

"Wow, girl, you are something out there."

Using a cocktail napkin to wipe the sweat on my forehead and face, I nodded. "Yeah, I do a little something when I have an able partner."

"Hmm, I haven't danced like that in ages. It felt good, though," he said. Melvin pulled his hankie from his pocket and grazed his face. He leaned in to bring his face closer to mine.

For the first time I noticed he looked like Prince. A bit taller and bigger, but he could've been Prince's twin. Minus that sexy mole, of course.

"I don't think I've seen you here before," he said.

"My first time," I glanced around to see if I could spot April. It was near impossible to see through the throng of people on the dance floor. The DJ was jamming and I started wiggling in my seat, chair dancing.

"Hmm, where do you hang out?" Melvin asked.

I scrunched up my face, shook my head, and pointed at my ears. I also started moving around more in the chair. He leaned in closer.

"I asked where you hang. You said this is your first time here."

I sighed, tilted my head, and looked at him. "I don't really go out like I used to. Folks always want to try and hold conversation. I come to a club to get my party on." I was hoping he'd take the hint.

Instead, he got up from the seat, moved his chair closer to mine and said, "I like you already."

Dexter

I'd been up most of the night flipping channels, watching a show here and there, but my mind was on Keisha. An hour after I got to Roger's apartment, I turned my cell back on and had checked my messages. There was only one message from Keisha.

Please, Dexter, come home. We need to talk about this, baby. This is not how we solve our problems. Please call me back. I can explain everything if you just give me a chance. I love you.

"What is there to explain?" I shouted at the phone. "You said you were in LA with April! Come to find out you were in Aruba!" I threw my phone on the couch. "In Aruba with God only knows who!"

I got up from the couch and paced back and forth. "Just give her a chance, she says. A chance for what? For her to make a fool of me." I went to the fridge and grabbed another beer. "'Call me,' she says. Well if you wanna talk, you can call me." I bounced down on the couch and grabbed the remote. "I'm tired of this shit!" I turned to CNN, but they were arguing about the war, and I had problems of my own. "If your ass wanna be single, then fuck it, be single!"

I changed the station to ESPN and watched Nascar like I actually cared what was going on. By the time I'd crushed my fifth beer can, I'd calmed down to the point that I was thinking more clearly. I heard Keisha's words again: *I can explain everything if you just give me a chance. I love you.*

"I love you, too, baby," I said and headed to the kitchen for another brew.

Several times during the night I resisted the urge to get up and go home. Each time I'd talk myself out of it, saying, *If she wants to talk, she can call me back.*

I don't know when I finally fell asleep, but the television was still on when I woke up. I wished I had fallen asleep in a better position. My lower back was killing me.

I opened my eyes to see Roger in his boxers, on the phone with his feet resting on the coffee table. "So if I wanted you to cook for me, a brotha would just be in serious trouble," he whispered into the phone.

I sat up and yawned. "What's up, Roger?" I said. I got up from the couch and made my way to the bathroom. When I came out, Roger was still on the phone. I have no idea when he came in. I looked at the clock on the wall; it was almost early morning. "I'm going to get something to eat," I said. "You hungry?"

"Hold on, baby." Roger put his hand over the phone. "Where you goin'?"

"Mickey D's."

"Bring me a sausage McMuffin with eggs and some hash browns. Oh, and a large coffee," Roger said and took his hand away from the door. "No, that ain't no woman. That's my boy Dexter. He left his wife last night. Say hello, Dee," Roger said and held up the phone.

"You don't have to put my business in the street," I said and walked out.

When I got back, Roger was still on the phone. I took the food into the small kitchen and flicked on the light. Roger only dealt with paper commodities. He had paper cups and plates and plastic utensils. I fixed my plate and left his on the counter so he could do the same.

When I walked back into the front room he was off the phone. He stared at my food like he hadn't eaten in weeks.

"Man, your food is in the kitchen," I said.

"Oh, cool. I just need to make another call first."

By the time he wrapped up that conversation I was on my second helping. I also realized from the one-way conversation, although he was hungry, food wasn't the only thing Roger was trying to scrape up. I wasn't sure if he had convinced anyone to come over, but after he ate, he turned his attention to my problematic marriage and me. "So dawg, has Keisha even called to see about you? I know she hasn't called while I've been here. What's up?"

"Nothing, man." I didn't really feel like having that conversation, especially not with him. I had never been one to sit and discuss my personal business, not just because my friends disliked my wife, but it wasn't my style.

Roger slowly nodded his head. He chuckled, "Nothing, huh?" he picked up his egg-Mac. "Well my sofa would say different. I mean you don't have to put your business out there if you don't want to but, just answer me this. She catch you and 'ole girl fuckin'?"

"What?" I yelled.

"Larry and me put some cash on it, man," Roger said with a straight face.

"You did what? You put money on me cheating on my wife?" I shook my head.

"It was Larry's idea. I just figured I'd take his $250. I mean if he just has money to throw away," Roger said.

"So what was your bet?" I asked.

"Dee, I just didn't see how you could live under the same roof as April's fine ass and not even think about hitting it."

"How long have you known me, Roger?" I asked.

He shook his head. "I know, man. I know. That's why I bet Larry it wasn't gonna happen," he laughed. "You know you my boy, right? And you know I know you." Roger laughed again. "But I gotta admit, when I saw you at my front door with your bags, man, I was speechless. All I could think was, *I'll be damned!*"

"So you thought I was kicked out for hitting on my wife's best friend?" I asked, still surprised.

"I didn't know what to think. Truthfully, I was really thinking about letting $250 slip through my fingers like water," he chuckled.

"It wasn't even anything like that. You know I wouldn't go out like that," I assured him.

"Yeah, I know, I know you're too nice for that kind of stuff, one of the good guys," Roger said mockingly.

I couldn't help but think, *Yeah, and we all know where the nice guys always finish.*

Last.

By Monday morning, Mama and Janet were blowing up my cell phone to the point that I considered answering just to say stop fuckin' calling. Each time it went off, I secretly prayed it would be Keisha, but it wasn't, and that shit only made me more determined not to call her ass.

I had to decide what I was going to do because I was getting tired of sleeping on Roger's couch. It made no sense that I had a big, sprawling four-bedroom house and here I was camped out in somebody's living room. At first I told myself it was the principle of the matter that had me so mad at Keisha. But the aches in my back told me I needed to rethink that.

Add that to the fact that Roger didn't know how to cook and we were constantly ordering food or eating out—I knew something needed to change. That, or I at least needed to make up with Mama and Janet, which I was not ready to do. My plan was to teach those two a lesson.

I didn't have to volunteer for overtime, but I figured that was my best option. The longer I worked, the less time I would have to sit alone and think about Keisha. By the time I left the job, it was close to ten Tuesday night. I was going to roll by the house, but I was really tired. I stopped and picked up some Boston Market for dinner and headed back to Roger's apartment to pack my things.

Keisha

The more I thought about my life, the more I wondered how I became the woman I am. I can remember the days of watching my mother get ready to go out with one of her many boyfriends, and wishing my turn would come fast. I used to love it. My mom would ask my advice about what to wear, which earrings or shoes looked best with which outfit, and I wanted nothing more than to be able to do the same one day.

While she'd have a date about four or five times a week, she would steady preach to me about the importance of a husband.

I would always say, "Mama, if a husband is so important, why don't you have one, and why are you always going out?"

My mom would stop getting ready for her date and look me dead in the eyes and say, "That's why I'm going out, so I can find a husband for me and a daddy for you."

She did eventually get that husband, but I was gone and off to college by then. So my only memories growing up were of her, getting ready to go out, and I guess you could say that's what stuck.

Being married to Dexter was about so much more than just proving Hattiemae and Janet, along with his two best friends, wrong. I wanted to be the woman my mother couldn't be. I wanted to have a happy and successful marriage. I didn't want to be up in the clubs at fifty, trying to compete with the young chicks. I wanted someone to grow old with.

I really was devastated about the breakup of my marriage. I was most shocked that he had left me, when it was me who alerted him to a problem in the first place. It's true, I didn't actually want us to be apart, I was just hoping my talk would do what it did at first, put him on alert, make him prove to me that I was worth hanging on to.

Even after he left, I really didn't want my marriage to end, but it would've been hard to tell, the way I was smiling all up in Melvin's handsome face.

By Monday I had expected to hear from Dexter. When Wednesday rolled around and passed with no word from him, I figured I might as well take Melvin up on his offer. He wanted to take April and me to dinner. He had already promised her she didn't have to be the third wheel, so she was hyped.

It seems the guy she was hugged up with in the corner Saturday night still hadn't called like he swore he'd do. She didn't tell me right away, but later I learned that she had sex with him before we even left the club.

"Keisha, what did Melvin say about his friend? Was he at the club with us?" April pressed. We were at the nail shop both getting spa pedicures.

"He didn't mention that, but I didn't ask, either."

"Well, what's his name again? I want to make sure I look real nice for him."

"His name is Robert. And just be yourself, I'm sure that'll be just fine."

April glanced my way as if I had just told a joke that wasn't funny.

"Well, not your self self. But the one who knows she's looking for a man." I went back to my old *Essence* magazine.

When we left the nail shop I was still a bit uneasy about dating. I wasn't sure what to do anymore. I mean, the last man I was with besides my husband took me in the backseat of his Hummer. While I knew that wasn't proper date protocol, I did wonder if I should tell Melvin about the status of my marriage. Then I wondered just what the status actually was. And what if I found him irresistible? *Do I kiss him? Do I allow him to kiss me?* It was so stressful just thinking about it all. It had only been a week since Dexter left. Not even a complete week, but I had never been one to sit home and wait on any man, husband or not.

I offered to drive so that April and I could get up and leave at any time if need be.

We agreed to go to this little Mexican restaurant right off I-10. I had passed it a dozen times and people always talked about how good, albeit expensive, their food was.

I was impressed when Melvin, dressed in a cream-colored linen shirt and matching slacks, walked to the hostess and said, "We have reservations for four. Johnson, Melvin Johnson?"

"Oh, yes, right this way," she said, ushering us past a line of waiting customers. I looked around, taking in the ambience.

For a Thursday, I thought the place was kind of

crowded. I noticed mariachis moving to each table and serenading couples. A jolt hit my heart and for an instant I wished it were Dexter and me instead of some man I picked up in a club.

Robert was so into April it was almost disgusting. He was a dark-skinned man with the whitest teeth I'd ever seen on a human. Robert actually had on a suit, his nails were manicured, and he carried a man purse. But April seemed to like it, and that was all that mattered.

At the table, Melvin pulled out my chair, and he and Robert waited for us to sit before they took their seats. The tables were lit with thick candles placed in hurricane holders.

The linen tablecloths were pink instead of the standard white. I have to admit, with the music not too far from our table and the dimmed lighting, the setting was so intimate it left me longing for my husband. Not the current Dexter I'd become bored with, but the old Dexter, when we first met.

"I'm so glad you ladies decided to join us tonight," Melvin said as if he and Robert were going to have dinner without us if we hadn't come.

I smiled politely. Robert and April were in their own world. I was just praying she didn't do anything to embarrass herself, or worse, me.

We started with appetizers and margaritas. I was glad because the alcohol helped take the edge off a bit. I didn't want to spend my entire night thinking about Dexter while I was with another man.

Halfway through dinner, it dawned on me. This was what was missing from my life. I felt free again. The way Melvin looked at me, like he wanted to clear the table, undress me, and devour me as the main entrée. It made me feel special.

He seemed genuinely interested in me. He wanted to know what it was like teaching and even asked about Dexter. I had told him we were separated, but failed to mention for only one week. At the time that just didn't seem important.

The table was big enough that I couldn't hear what Robert and April were whispering about, but it didn't take long to see that they were hitting it off.

"I need to use the restroom," I said.

Ever the gentleman, Melvin rose from his chair and attempted to pull mine out. Of course, since I was not used to such treatment, he wasn't able to do his thing. But just knowing he wanted to was refreshing and impressive enough for me.

Robert jumped from his seat when he noticed me standing. April looked up at me like I had interrupted something really special. Still, she followed me to the ladies room.

"I think this is it!" she cried excitedly as soon as the door closed behind us.

"What?" I asked.

"Robert. He's the real thing. I just feel it, Keisha. I know I've been wrong about this sort of thing before, but there's just something real different about him." April's eyes were sparkling, and I hadn't seen her smile like this since she'd returned. She was genuinely excited.

I didn't want to burst her bubble by saying everyone, herself included, was on their very best behavior in the beginning. So I just let her go on about how much of a gentleman Robert was. She said he was in commercial real estate and owned a home on Galveston Island.

"Well, I hope you're right," I said to April.

"Girl, I think I am," she turned to the mirror to finish smoothing powder over her face. "You see the way they get up when we need to leave the table. And they pulled out our chairs. I can tell," she said, shaking her head. Suddenly, she stopped fixing her makeup and turned to me, "Ooooh, and that Melvin looks like he's really into you, too," she offered, as if I needed a consolation prize since she had finally gotten a winner.

When I looked in the mirror, my reflection screamed, "What the hell are you doing? You are married!"

Dexter

It had been a week since I walked out on my wife. Since then there had been a battle raging between my brain and my heart. I had no idea which would win, but I knew something had to change soon. I couldn't stay there taking her shit and sitting around like a chump.

My brain told me I was doing the right thing. But my heart said I needed to go back home. But, more important, my pride said I'd be the biggest sucker in H-town if I just went sulking back to her.

The summer was almost over and Keisha would be going back to work soon. Even though I was away from her and home, I never imagined our fight would last this long. When I thought about it, I was more than a little hurt because this was a sign that, given the choice, she'd choose her old life with April over what we had built.

I knew sooner or later I was going to have to talk to Keisha, even if that meant just going over there. After all, it was my house. I paid the mortgage there, which was one more reason why I couldn't be at a motel. I'd talked myself into and out of going over there so many times. Both Keisha and I were prideful and stubborn people. One of us would have to give in, and I felt very strongly that it could be her.

I have to admit that it hurt me that Keisha hadn't even made another attempt to call me. Even if she didn't want us to be together, I thought that I meant enough to at least merit a "how you doing" call. I tried not to think about it and buried myself in work.

One night when I was getting ready to leave work, Penny, one of my co-workers, walked slowly into the office, kind of lifelessly. She plopped down in the chair and exhaled very deeply. I looked at her eyes. She didn't look tired, but it was almost as though she was dragging herself. That was out of character for her, because Penny never got tired. I'd seen her go two days in the office without sleep. By the end of the second day all of us were done, but not Penny. She was trying to lead us in a sing-along of "We Are The World."

"What's up, Penny?" I asked and continued getting ready to leave.

"I don't wanna go home," she said.

"Why not?"

"Just a little frustrated with my husband, that's all."

"Really, what's wrong?" I asked. Penny had never discussed her personal business with me before. I hadn't told her, or anybody else for that matter, that I had walked out on my wife. So it was a little strange that she would be coming to me with it now.

"He doesn't pay me any attention. We don't do anything together."

"Y'all don't watch television together?"

"When we watch TV, yeah, we're in the same room, but we're not together. He sits in his chair. I sit on the couch and that's that. It's like we're strangers sometimes."

I thought about me and Keisha doing the exact same thing. "You don't think he's fooling around on you, do you?" I asked, thinking Keisha could've been confiding in someone the same way.

"No. Well, at least I don't think so. I mean, when would he have time? I could set a clock by him. He leaves the house the same time every morning, gets home the same time every night. He never goes anywhere. He doesn't have anybody he hangs out with. No one ever calls him, except his family from Tennessee. I try to get him to go out after work with the guys he works with, but he won't go."

"Y'all don't go anywhere together? Have a drink, catch a flick, nothing? Go to a restaurant? Nothing like that?" I was surprised to learn that maybe I hadn't been the only homebody in Houston.

"If I don't cook, we'll go eat."

"That's pretty bad."

"Fucked up is what it is," Penny said, slumping lower in her chair.

I never knew it was like that. I felt bad for her. Penny was one of the nicest people I knew. Everybody liked her, always so alive and friendly. I never would have thought that she was that unhappy. Or was she? "How does that make you feel?" I asked like a psychologist.

"You want me to go lie down on the couch?" Penny joked, as she started to get up.

"Sit down, girl, it ain't that type o' party."

"I was about to say, since you trying to psychoanalyze me." We both laughed. Then Penny got up and walked toward the window. "I tried talking to him about it. But he doesn't think there's anything wrong. He says, 'It ain't like we argue.' And he's right, we don't. But sometimes I wish we did. Maybe then, he'd show me some passion."

"Hey," I said, pointing a cautioning finger. "Be careful what you wish for." It felt like she was talking to me about me.

"You're right. I sure don't wanna go there. But a little emotion would be nice. A little emotion directed at me would be better. Just a little bit of passion, maybe. What am I saying, a whole lot of passion. I don't think that's a whole lot for a wife to ask of her husband. When I called Ike to tell him that I had to work late, you know what he said?"

"I'm afraid to ask."

"Did you cook? That's all he had to say, not 'what time will you be home?' not 'I'll miss you,' not 'I'll wait up for you.' Just some fuckin' food, like it doesn't matter whether I was there or not. I might as well sleep on the couch. We barely have sex anymore and when we do, after I beg, I should say, it's so mechanical."

I didn't comment on that one.

"Dexter, most nights we just go to sleep. No touching, no kissin', just sleep. And when he does give me what I call 'pity dick,' it's like he's running a race or something. Like he's in a hurry to get it over with, and when he's done, that's it. No regard whatsoever for me. He don't care whether I get mine or not. It's very frustrating."

"Maybe you should try making it more exciting for him. Wear something sexy? Tempt him, tease him, make him want you."

"Been there, done that. Something sexy, huh. If you only knew, Dexter." She laughed, "If you only knew."

I laughed, didn't know why, but I laughed. "If I only

knew what, Penny?" She walked back to the chair and sat down. Then she smiled at me.

"If you only knew what I had on under these jeans and this blouse."

"What?"

"Let's just say it's black and lacy."

"Oooh." My eyebrows inched up. I was curious.

"I like wearing lingerie. I got tons of it. Victoria's Secret, Frederick's of Hollywood, all that. I love it."

"Oh, really." I never thought she went in for stuff like that. She always seemed so plain, dressed in pants every day. I seemed to remember her having nice legs when I hired her, but that was the last time I saw them. I guess you never really know.

"Does that surprise you? Never mind. I can tell by that look in your eyes. You didn't think I was the sexy lingerie type. Well I am, big-time."

"He doesn't like you in it?" I was getting all caught up in her world.

"He used to. I guess it got old, common, you know what I mean?"

"Try something else," I suggested.

"What do you have in mind? I've tried everything I can think of."

"Like what?" Now I was curious. Just how far had she gone. Penny was an attractive woman. What Roger would call a nice piece of business, a little on the bony side for my personal taste, but attractive. You wouldn't think she'd have to go through no whole group of changes just to get her freak on. But what did I know.

"I've tried everything. From nasty movies, to serving him a candlelit dinner naked. Nothing about it seems to get him excited. Nothing about me excites him. I'm twenty-nine years old, I need to feel like a woman. I need to feel wanted. And I don't. And I hate it," Penny said, once again slumping deep in the chair.

"Wow, I'm sorry to hear that." What else could I say?

I was ready to go. She was starting to depress me. My relationship with Keisha wasn't that bad. I couldn't be in such a rush to throw it away. I considered Penny a friend and she was baring her soul to me. I felt like I had to hear her out. The last thing she needed was for me to seem disinterested or that I didn't care, either.

I looked at my watch and leaned my head back. I sat there with my eyes closed, listening without really hearing. Waiting for my spot to say, "I gotta go," when Penny said, "I just need to feel desirable." Then she ran her hand down my crotch.

I jumped up and moved around to my side of the desk.

"But you don't want me, either. Do you?"

I started to yell "HELL NO," as I put my jacket on. Once I got it on, I took a deep breath and tried to regain my composure.

"Penny, you know I'm married and I love Keisha." I started walking around the desk to leave. "I can't say that I love her and do her like that. Can't you understand that?"

"She doesn't have to know," Penny said, as she moved to cut me off at the corner of the desk.

"I'll know. And that's the same thing."

"I'm sorry, Dexter," she smiled at me, like the cat that swallowed the chicken. "I don't know what came over me."

It wasn't what she said, it was the way she said it, like it really didn't bother her at all. The look in her eyes told a different story than the one coming out of her mouth.

"No, it was my fault. I got a little carried away."

"I think we both did," she said smiling, backing out of my office slowly.

We both laughed about it and agreed it shouldn't have happened and that it would never happen again. Both of us got our things quietly and left. On the way back to the motel I thought about what had just happened. How I should never have put myself in that position. The guilt came down on me hard then.

Keisha

August 20 marked two full weeks since Dexter left, and I still hadn't heard a peep out of him. I knew he was going to work every day because I had called a few times and hung up when he answered.

I secretly wondered how long things would last the way they were. Suddenly it dawned on me that I was preparing myself, at least mentally, for a long-term breakup. It didn't help that Melvin had become a fixture in my life.

We had seen each other three times since dinner, and he had bought tickets for us to see a concert together Saturday night at the Toyota Center. I wasn't sure if I was trying to move on, but I couldn't deny the way Melvin made me feel.

A few days ago, he invited me to dinner at his loft downtown. He sent a car to pick me up because he didn't want me to have to drive out to Katy late at night and he had an early meeting the next morning.

When I stepped out to the waiting black town car, I felt so special and important. I was wearing a light purple chiffon spaghetti-strapped dress that flowed with each step I took. I had my hair swooped to one side with a baby iris stuck at my ear.

Riding in the backseat of that car, I felt like a different woman. Never would Dexter and I consider doing anything on a Wednesday night. It wasn't because of me, but him. He'd fuss about having to go to work the next day and after all of the complaining, I wouldn't want to do anything, either.

The driver pulled up in front of Melvin's building and I felt like a princess. There was even a doorman! I didn't know what the proper protocol was for this type of situation. So I tried to tip them both, but they declined to accept, which made me feel even more out of place.

As I rode the elevator up to Melvin's floor, I kept reminding myself that I was still, in fact, a married woman. When I stepped into his place, my heart practically stopped beating. Rose petals were scattered all over.

The living room was furnished with an oversized sofa, a sixty-inch plasma-screen TV, and two wing chairs. The wood floors reminded me of ours at home; they glowed beneath a dark stain. Expensive Oriental rugs were spread throughout various rooms.

I didn't smell any food, but soft music flooded the room and added to the intimate atmosphere Melvin had already created. It took my mind off my empty stomach. The lights cast a peach hue over everything. I never would've thought to use colored lightbulbs, but he had and it worked.

He suddenly appeared, wearing a pair of black slacks and a thin, but snug, deep olive green silk shirt. It showed off the muscles in his thin frame. I couldn't help but mentally compare him and the things he did to Dexter.

"You look breathtaking this evening," he said. "Was the ride over okay?"

I nodded.

"Relax, kick off your shoes, you might as well be at home," he assured me.

I think he could see in my eyes that I was questioning being there. He reached out and rubbed my shoulders. His bare hands felt so good gliding against my skin.

"I'll be right back," he said. I walked down the three steps that led to his living room and looked around. He had artwork tastefully scattered throughout, with a massive book collection. His place looked classy and sophisticated.

When he reappeared, he was holding two wine goblets. "Chardonnay," he said, as he sipped from one and passed me the other.

"Thanks." I quickly gulped nearly half of it down without thinking. When I realized how I had guzzled down the drink, I felt a bit embarrassed.

Melvin looked and chuckled a bit. "Relax," he said. Then he led me by the hand. "Let me show you the rest of the place."

As we walked down a short hallway, he said, "This is the hall." He smiled. "To your right," he pushed a door, "is the gym." I glanced in and nodded. Across from there, he pushed another door. "This is guest bedroom number one," he said.

We came back the way we had gone after he showed me the second guest bedroom and bathrooms. The spiral staircase led to a wide-open space that contained his bedroom. His king-sized bed sat on a pedestal, the type of stuff you only saw in movies. The bed was all but calling my name. I knew then that I should've declined the tour.

When he pressed a button and a blue light slowly lit the room, I was simply in awe. His taste in clothes and everything else absolutely fascinated me. Melvin was smooth.

"The blue light special of course," he chuckled. The next switch he hit automatically drew thick drapes back to reveal a set of French doors that spilled out to a balcony.

I was drawn to it right away. I moved closer to the doors and stood near enough to have my nose pressed against the glass like a kid who was window-shopping. Noticing that, Melvin was on my heels as I tried not to overreact. "You like that?" he asked, speaking softly.

He dimmed the blue light, then unlocked the door. We walked out onto the balcony, which I never imagined was as large as it was.

As we walked around to another section, I noticed a small table set with plates and silverware. A tall silver ice bucket stood nearby. Candles flickered in hurricane glasses.

I could just imagine the look of sheer shock that must've been spread across my face when I turned to look at him.

"I hope you're hungry," he said.

We enjoyed dinner on the terrace—too big to be considered a balcony—and even danced a few times. I was in heaven.

Unfortunately, I had to follow him back into the blue bedroom.

"We don't have to do anything you don't feel comfortable doing," he pressed. "But I think you could use a massage to help you relax a bit." He motioned for me to stretch out on the bed. I hesitated at first, but he nodded, urging me to trust him.

I eased onto his bed, and lay on my stomach. When his powerful hands traveled across my bare shoulders, I felt electricity in his touch. His strokes were strong and firm, yet soothing.

"I'm a certified masseur," he tempted me.

I turned my head to look back at him skeptically. He shrugged. "Okay, well not really, but I might as well be. I've been told I'm just that good," he confessed with a slighter shrug.

His hands traveled from my shoulders to the middle of my back. I was embarrassed when I realized the soft moaning sound filling the room was actually coming from me.

As I lay on my stomach, Melvin unzipped my dress and continued to work on the knots in my neck, shoulders, and muscles.

I felt his hardness when he climbed on my lower back to rub my neck and shoulders better. I had already decided to give myself to him, but I wanted to reap all of the benefits before I completely succumbed.

Satisfied that my back was completely relaxed, and without signs of stress, I willfully turned over. This, I told myself, was what I had been missing—pure and simple romance. *If only Dexter could* . . . "Aaahh."

When Melvin pulled the strings at my hips that held my thong together, I closed my eyes and gave myself permission to enjoy whatever might be coming next.

He sucked my hip like honey had dripped there and his sole job was to sop it up. Who would've ever thought a hip bone was an erotic zone? But the way Melvin worked my flesh with his tongue, I wanted to see what else that tongue of his could do.

As his tongue flickered across my skin, I felt a tantalizing flood threatening to burst through my thighs.

"Oh, Melvin," I cried, and he still hadn't moved from my hip. He stroked me, touching me to the core and I know I was emitting warmth and eagerness.

I don't know if he was done tasting my hip, but I spread my legs, proving that I wanted whatever he had to offer, and alerting him, he could have my best.

It must've taken him a minute to realize what I was saying, but when he did, Melvin pulled away so he could look me dead in my eyes and said, "Are you sure?"

I just wanted him to take me before I lost my nerve. When I nodded, he moved toward me, nearly gulping my breast in the process. He kneaded my chest with such power and passion I started to come right then and there.

"Sssss, you make me feel so . . ."

"Ssshh, you should always feel this way," he cut me off before diving between my thighs. When his tongue made contact with my slippery pearl, everything slowed down instantly. He didn't quite suck it, he just used his tongue to add pressure to my panic button. I threw my head back and squeezed my eyes shut. I rubbed his head, caressing the sides of his neck and shoulders. I didn't want him to stop.

Melvin behaved like it was his mission to make me wet, then suck me dry.

When he pulled back to look at me, I struggled not to scream, but I did manage to grab his head, helping to guide him right back to my most sensitive spot until I literally cried out with satisfaction.

He eased up, licking his lips and fingers as if he didn't want to risk wasting a single drop of my fluids. He savored my flavor and continued the body massage that forced me to submit.

Just when I thought it couldn't get any better, he entered me and completely took my breath away, filling every inch of my tunnel with penetrating precision.

"Oh, Melvin," I sang his name, keeping up with his wicked strokes. We moved in sync as if we'd been loving each other forever.

Dexter

It was Saturday night, and me and Roger were sitting around with nothing to do. I didn't have to work the next day, so I was game for whatever he had in mind. He wanted to go to a sports bar to watch a game, and I figured we might as well. Otherwise, I'd sit there and think about Keisha.

My plan was to go to the sports bar with Roger, we'd enjoy the game, and hang out a bit. We went in separate cars just in case I was ready to leave early. What I wasn't expecting was, the place Roger took us to was crawling with women.

Fine women.

The minute we hit the bar and got a table, Roger invited two women to join us. When I tried to protest, Roger whispered, "It gonna be right, Dee. We just talkin' damn."

"I'm married," I felt the need to say to the honey-colored woman with the pretty smile. Her name was Vanessa and she was wearing a red dress that looked pretty short. Since she was sitting down, I couldn't tell how short. She sat with her legs crossed, which forced me to notice her nice, thick thighs.

Vanessa didn't try to disguise the disappointment that spread across her face when I said I was married.

"Separated," Roger corrected.

I saw a light of hope in Vanessa's eyes and I didn't have the heart to kill it, especially since her friend and Roger seemed to be getting along quite well.

By the time I finished my second Long Island Ice Tea, I was feeling pretty good. For the most part, I watched the game while Roger talked with the ladies. Every once in a while I'd dip into the conversation to answer a question, when asked, or to comment on something, but for the most part, I wasn't in the mood for a whole lot of talking.

By the time I finished my third Long Island, my judgment was impaired and I was feeling no pain. In simpler terms, I was drunk and so was Vanessa. She was knocking down gin and juice like it was water. We weren't sloppy, stumbling-over-our-words drunk, but we were both pretty far out there. When Kim, the woman Roger was talking to, suggested we move the party to her place, I really wasn't up for it. "I'd like to, but I'm actually about to go home and beg my wife to take me back," I said.

"Awwww," the women sang in unison.

Roger's eyes were wide with horror. He started frowning. "I need to holla' at you for a minute, Dee." He turned to the ladies. "Don't move, stay right here. Order another drink, and we'll be right back."

When Roger got me to the back of the bar, he said, "Man, what's wrong with you?"

"What are you talkin' about?" I asked.

"Why are you tryin' to fuck this up?"

"I ain't trying to do anything. I'm just not interested in moving the party to her place," I said.

"Dee, man, come on. I'm not saying you should cheat on your wife, but dawg, you haven't even talked to her in days."

"Doesn't matter, I'm still married, and I'm not about to sleep with a woman I just met just so you could get at her friend. I'm not even willing to entertain the idea."

"Come on, Dee, just hang out with me. Nobody's gonna force you to fuck her. Just go over there and talk. The two of you been sittin' over there talkin' all night. Just keep talkin' to Vanessa about whatever the fuck she wanna talk about, while I talk up on Kim's pussy."

"Okay, I'll go with you," I was just tired of listening to his ass beg.

"Dee, that's why you my boy." Roger gave me a hug. "Let's go get *me* some pussy."

When we got to Kim's place, the party continued just as it had been at the sports bar. The only major differences were, we were all drinking gin and juice and Roger and Kim were in her living room on the couch. They were all up in each other's faces, while Vanessa and I sat at the dining room table, talking. We were all getting pretty drunk.

"What you thinking so hard about over there?" Vanessa asked.

"Thinking hard about you." If she only knew just how hard I was thinking about her and how hard those thoughts were getting me. If I really wanted to be honest with myself, I found Vanessa to be very attractive. She was nice, easy to talk to. I was proud of myself: since I announced that I was married, I hadn't said a word about Keisha all night. Come to think of it, I really hadn't thought much about her at all. "Thinking about getting out of here while I can still walk," I answered the same question again.

"You ain't drunk are you?"

"No, not drunk, but I definitely got my buzz on."

"Good, 'cause I was thinking the same thing."

"Oh, really." I smiled and leaned close to her. Close enough to smell the gin on her breath, not to mention close enough to get a real good look at her cleavage.

"That's not what I'm thinking about. . . ."

"How do you know what I'm thinking about?" I said and sat back in my chair.

"Hello! It's that 'I wanna fuck you so bad it hurts' look. It's written all over your face. I may have my buzz on, too, but I'm not blind."

"Damn . . . Am I that obvious?"

"No more than any other man. Besides, we got plenty of time for all that belly to belly stuff." Vanessa finished her drink and looked around. "Anyway, I was thinking about gettin' out of here. I really don't wanna bother Kim. You wouldn't mind taking me home in that big 'ole SUV of yours? What you think about that?"

"Sounds like a real plan to me."

As we approached the interstate, she was really riding me. "Let's see what this bad boy can do," Vanessa said. "That is, if you can."

"What do you mean, if I can?"

"I didn't stutter. I mean if you can. You may be having some problems working your stick." It wasn't so much what she said, it was the way she said it. Like just about everything she said, it was laced with sexual innuendo. I turned the truck hard and fast and headed out on I-10 and started to weave through traffic.

"That's what I'm talking about. Speed!" she screamed.

"Never let it be said that I couldn't handle my stick, Boo."

"Yeah. I'd be very interested to see." She reached over and rubbed my hand on the stick as I dropped it down a gear. Vanessa ran her hand up and down my arm. "Yeah, I'd be very interested to see just how well you handle your stick. I hate when a man gets me all worked up for a nice long ride and he can't really handle his stick."

"You like to ride, huh?"

"Long, hard ride, matter of fact, it's one of my favorite things."

"What else do you like?" I asked, as her hand moved to my thigh and she squeezed it.

"I could show you better then I could tell you," Vanessa replied, rubbing my thigh, inching ever so close.

"I just bet you can."

"Hey, hey, get off here."

I complied with her request and got off at the next exit. I didn't ask why. I didn't care. As we passed the Fairfield Inn, Vanessa said, "Pull over here."

I turned into the parking lot and parked in front of the office.

"Why don't you go get us a room, handsome."

"I'll be right back." I quickly got out of the car and went inside to handle my assigned task. Once we got to the room, I tried to kiss her right away. "Slow down, handsome. We got plenty of time for all that," she said and pulled a half pint of Alizé out of her purse. "Why don't you go get some ice so we can have a drink?"

I composed myself.

It wasn't easy.

I grabbed the bucket and went for the ice. When I got

back to the room, the lights were out. The room was lit only by the television, with no sound. The radio was on and the shower was running. I casually fixed the drinks in the hotel-issued plastic cups and got undressed. Then I grabbed the cups and went into the bathroom. I pulled back the shower curtain and joined her. She was a little caught off guard by my sudden appearance. I handed the cup to her and we stood there sipping Alizé and looking each other up and down. I didn't know about her, but I was thoroughly impressed with what was standing before me. And my impression was obvious.

"Hmm," she said. "I hope you taste as good as you look." She proceeded to pour Alizé across my chest and it quickly dripped down to my impression. She ran her tongue across my nipples and worked her way down to my impression. And then she proceeded to take it all in.

I was in ecstasy.

I grabbed the curtain rod to steady myself.

After what seemed like an eternity, we got out of the shower. We slowly dried one another off, both of us exploring the other's body, with the towel, our hands, and our eyes.

It didn't take long for me to start exploring with my tongue, until I felt her body jerk. I grabbed her thighs and sucked even harder. She started smacking me all about the head and shoulders, and I kept holding on to that magic button that had her climbing the walls.

She came so hard and loud, I thought our neighbors would soon be knocking on the wall to quiet us down. Once done, I eased up and sat next to her on the bed. "Lie on your back, let me do you," she said.

I smiled my reply and again quickly complied with her wishes. Vanessa knelt on the bed next to me. She leaned forward and kissed me. She moved from side to side, rubbing her chest across mine, in beat with the music. The sensation I felt when I felt her nipples rub against mine was indescribable. I ran my hands down her back and across her cheeks, as she started to move her hips faster. Then Vanessa sat up and went to work. After a while she stopped and moved her legs so her feet were on the bed. Then she proceeded to fuck the shit out of me.

We'd stop from time to time, to catch our breath, have a drink, and talk some shit. A couple of times we just stopped and sat there, breathing hard, staring at each other and shaking our heads.

Keisha

When the limo pulled up in front of my house after the concert, April leaned over and whispered, "I'm not staying here tonight. I'm going back to Robert's." She giggled like we shared a common secret.

I felt kind of odd. I hated to admit it, but I didn't want to go into that big empty house all alone. Melvin must've sensed my hesitation. When he got out to walk me to the door, he touched my chin.

"You okay? You have a good time tonight?"

I nodded.

"This evening doesn't have to end," he said. I was hopeful, but didn't want to come off desperate.

"Why don't I tell the driver to drop them off and swing back by for me afterwards," he offered.

I was already feeling better. I watched as he walked back to the limo. When he came back to me, he paused a bit.

"I need to warn you," he said. "I won't be held responsible for what might happen in there," he chuckled.

"C'mon inside," I said, hoping none of my nosy

neighbors were up late. I should've felt guilty about having another man all up in my house, but recently I had begun preparing for life alone again. I had told myself we just needed to work out the details. The more time I spent with Melvin, the more I started to believe my marriage was just as good as over. Dexter was making his intentions really loud and clear.

I hadn't tried to call him again. I felt like I had done my part. I did feel uneasy when Melvin passed our bedroom. I knew I couldn't give him the kind of tour he had extended to me, and I think he kind of understood. Never once did he complain.

Melvin looked around the formal living and dining rooms. "A person's home says a lot about them," he told me.

"Oh? So what's my place saying about me?" I wasn't about to show him anything that wasn't already visible, but I did want him to feel comfortable, so we moved the conversation to the family room.

"Well, I'm getting mixed messages."

"Oh really?"

"Yeah, the furniture, wood floors, rugs all say someone who's reserved, tamed." He looked around the room. "But the pictures, of your soon-to-be ex, I assume. Well, they show a bit of a wild streak. The sand in the urn, adventure," he said.

I shook my head at him playfully. "Would you like a drink?" I asked. I wondered why he assumed Dexter was my soon-to-be ex. Then I remembered the last time I was at his place. Just the mere thought of my behavior embarrassed me to no end. I wasn't sure what was going on with Melvin and me.

He was everything I could want in a man. He was romantic, generous, fun, and spontaneous. He was everything I wanted Dexter to be. I told myself that I would not sleep with him again. It wasn't fair to him, Dexter, or me.

I poured two glasses of wine. Our fingers touched when Melvin took his from me. I tried to ignore what I felt, reminding myself that I didn't need to sleep with him again until I decided what I was going to do about Dexter.

My alone time with Melvin made Dexter more of a distant memory. My warped mind kept telling me that Melvin was the type of man I should've married, especially when he put on the music and started moving his hips seductively.

"Why are you trying to start something?" I asked.

"What, you can't handle it, Miss Dancing Queen?"

"I know what you're up to and it's not going to work," I said as I walked to the family room to get a better look at his moves.

Melvin was downright sexy. No question about it. I felt myself fighting back desire.

"I will never do anything you don't want done. Remember that," he said, before spinning and shaking his hips.

I kept my eyes on him. The way he moved while dancing made me wonder why he was still single. I also wondered if he was only behaving this way because we weren't a bona fide couple.

"What's on your mind?" he stopped dancing and came to me.

"Nothing," I lied.

"Oh, it's something. But you don't have to share if you don't want," he sipped his wine.

Melvin slid off the sofa and spread my legs. On his knees he came within inches of my face. "Look, I know you've got some things to work through. I'm not trying to rush you one way or the other. I enjoy your company.

We have fun together. I want whatever you can give me, even if you decide to go back to him," he said, nodding toward the large picture of Dexter and me.

"What does that mean?" I needed to know.

"Let's be real, Keisha. You've been married for five years. If it was truly over between you and your husband, you'd be divorced already. People only separate when they're not sure what to do. If you guys decide to divorce, I won't crowd you. Who knows? Maybe after five years you just want to test the waters again. You might be trying to not get tied down again." He shrugged.

I wondered how he could just nonchalantly sum up my situation in such meaningless phrases. He made it sound easy. My options were, either Dexter, with him on the side, or no Dexter and him occasionally. I wondered if there was a small camera somewhere. Someone had to be taping this, a test like what had happened to April in LA, because it made no sense to me that a fine, wealthy man like Melvin would be willing to settle for so little.

"So you're saying I could keep my husband and still have you?" I just needed to get things straight.

"What I'm saying is, I'd be a fool to think that man is out of your system entirely. But we click. We enjoy the same things. It's hard to find those traits in a husband or a wife. No pressure from me, but I'm just telling you, before you drop me to go back to him, know that you have options."

Melvin took me into his arms. My shoulders convulsed against his chest, and I had to fight the urge to cry. I was so glad when the doorbell rang.

Then I remembered, I did have another man in my and my husband's house, and that was way outta order.

Dexter

I finally broke down and told Mama and Janet it was probably over between Keisha and me. I should've waited before saying anything to those two, but my depression over the situation had all but swallowed me.

We were at dinner when Mama glanced over and said I wasn't looking good. She wanted to know what Keisha had said about what she and Janet had done.

"I never got the chance to talk to her about it," I confessed.

"Why not?" Janet wanted to know. Soon I was under their microscope and I regretted having said anything at all. In fact, I regretted agreeing to meet them for dinner in the first place.

"So you still haven't talked to your wife?" Mama wanted to know. If she tried, she didn't do a good job of hiding her joy.

"It's just over," I said firmly.

I noticed them exchanging glances. Victory was written all over their faces. I'll bet Mama couldn't wait to call Pauline and set up another dinner. I, on the other hand, was thinking about the breakup of my marriage.

I knew that eventually I'd have to go to Keisha and we'd have to sit down and figure out how we'd handle things.

My mind didn't want to focus on any of that. I wanted to eat the food Mama had prepared and run back to my motel room. There I could mourn the death of my relationship in peace. But they wouldn't leave well enough alone.

"So should we go over there?" Mama asked.

I looked up at her. "Who is we? And should we go where?" I asked with building frustration.

"Well, I don't think she should be allowed to remain in that house another minute until we talk to our lawyers," Mama snapped.

"We could call Dickey Swanson," Janet offered all too cheerfully.

"I don't think *we* need to call anyone. I will handle this on my own." I looked at my sister with evil eyes and got up. "And, no, *we* are not going to put Keisha out of her home," I said firmly.

"We just want to protect your interests," Mama added, a little more subdued. I took a deep breath and tried to calm myself.

"I know, but *I* need to handle this. Besides, if Keisha agrees to go to counseling, I won't even need to worry about a divorce lawyer."

Neither of them even tried to mask the look of horror that had crossed their faces.

Keisha

I sat in the massive Jacuzzi tub in my bathroom and pondered how I could ever repair my life. Things seemed so hopeless.

April and I weren't partying as much because she had found what she called a "prospect." I wasn't jealous, but I did see the irony in the situation. When my marriage was good, I couldn't stay out of the clubs with her. But the minute she hooked up with someone for more than one night, she didn't want to be bothered with the club scene. And just my luck, she had this epiphany just when I was once again finding solace in hitting the clubs.

April had only been to the house one day last week. Melvin was away on business that week. He had even asked if I wanted to join him. I told him I didn't think it was a good idea, as I was feeling more and more guilty. He promised he'd call once he returned from Philadelphia.

I was in the kitchen going through the freezer in search of dinner when April walked in.

"Hey girl, what's going on?"

"Nothing much, school just started and I'm already wondering when it's gonna be over," I said as I pulled a rice bowl dinner out, frowned at it, and tossed it back.

"Don't worry about fixing anything for me. I'm not hungry," she said.

Not that I was thinking about feeding her anyway, but I guess it was good to know.

"Hey, why don't we go catch happy hour somewhere? I could go for some Mexican food and margaritas." I turned away from the freezer.

"Emmm," she wrinkled her nose.

"What, you and Robert hooking up tonight or something?" I asked because the two had been nearly inseparable lately.

"Nah, it's not that." She hesitated.

"Well? What is it? This is only the second time I've wanted to go out and you're sitting up acting like you have something better to do. What gives?"

"Well, I know with us happy hour usually turns into a night of clubbing." She shrugged and twisted up her face.

"Yeah, and that's never been a problem for you before," I reminded.

She sighed, "It's Robert, really. He says he doesn't like me being all up in the club, says it's not ladylike, and I don't know, I guess I kind of agree," she admitted softly.

"Oh, I see." I went back to the freezer.

"He took me shopping last week. He seems to think I could be more effective if I dressed, I don't know, more my age?" she asked more than said.

At that, I turned to see if April was serious. From the day I've known her, she had always dressed one step above a streetwalker, and wore her clothes like she was proud to be able to. That had been an April Perry trademark. I wasn't sure why she was trying to be more effective, but one thing seemed quite clear. If Robert says, then April does.

"Why don't we call and order some take-out. You've been in that freezer for a minute now, ain't nothing gonna appear if you haven't found it by now," she said. "Besides, I could go for something light."

"I guess you're right. Let's get some Chinese," I watched her while she went through the menu drawer.

April seemed different. Her hair was growing out, as was the blond color she used to sport. She was no longer wearing tons of gaudy jewelry and I looked at the shorts that stopped at her knees instead of at her cheeks.

"Uh, why are you wearing Bermuda shorts, April?"

"Girl, these are not Bermudas." She smoothed out the shorts with her hand. "I told you Robert took me shopping last week. He said he saw an episode of Oprah last week, and apparently she said these are the only kind of shorts women should wear." April looked down at her legs. "Besides, those little Daisy Dukes I made famous, well it really was time to hang them up."

I couldn't contain my shock. I didn't know why I hadn't noticed the subtle changes prior to our conversation. But in fact, April had changed, or at least she was putting on a good front. Either way, that left me to fend for myself.

Thoughts of her change made me think of my own. After my separation from Dexter, April and I were in the clubs from Tuesday through Sunday. At times we'd catch Monday night football at a sports bar. Back then, I believed life was finally back to the way I thought it should be.

Now, I'm soaking in the tub on a Friday night, the

music is on, but doesn't sound the same. April is with her man while *I'm* the one who's alone. I could've been with Melvin, but I had a long talk with myself and decided I needed to get off the fence. It was like one leg was dangling in the single life I had longed for and the other was in this uncertain marriage.

Dexter had called a few times, but I didn't have the heart to speak to him or return his phone calls. I guess at times I felt ashamed. I didn't know how to verbalize all that I had done. The reality of the situation was that I had turned into exactly what everyone had warned him against when it came to me.

At first this new relationship I had started with another man made me think I had found something better, but I wasn't sure anymore.

My skin was wrinkled when I finally stepped out of the tub. I used my Victoria's Secret lotion to lather my body, then followed up with perfumed oil. I sprayed the tub with cleanser, then picked out a pair of lounging pajamas.

There were several new releases on DVD and I had a date to catch up with at least two of them. I put on a pair of slipper socks and made my way out to the family room.

I nearly fell out when I saw Dexter standing there.

Dexter

I didn't know what Keisha would say or think, but I needed answers. When I pulled up to the house and saw her car in the driveway, I told myself there was no turning back this time.

I was determined to get something out of her when I walked up to the door. When I heard soft music coming from our room, it felt like déjà vu all over again, but I was still determined. I unlocked the door and quietly allowed myself inside.

I looked around the darkened house and immediately began missing home. I strolled through the formal living and dining rooms, remembering our times together. I missed my wife so much.

Before building up the courage to come over, I had already told myself I didn't care what happened while we were apart. I, after all, had been the one who left, and let's not forget my little indiscretion. I just wanted Keisha back.

April could even stay, but we'd have to work on an exit plan for her. I didn't want an indefinite houseguest. Not to mention a broke one. I noticed the change in our savings account since she had been back, but I didn't say anything. I was just determined to get April Perry out of our life. If it meant me paying rent on an apartment for two months, I'd do it for peace of mind in my home.

With my mind made up, I passed near our room, and that's when I heard the sounds. My wife was in the tub, humming to slow jams and no one else was there. I was thrilled.

Instead of bursting in there and surprising her, I used the time to think of what I'd say when she came out.

"Baby, I'm home?" Nah, that wouldn't work.

"Can I come back home?" I whispered. I shook my head and started thinking about the worst-case scenario. What if she looked at me and wondered why I had even come back? What if she was enjoying the single life? Maybe I should've taken a hint. I called her at school, at home, and on her cell phone. She never returned a single call.

Could it be that she really was tired of our life? What if we'd both changed so much that we were no longer compatible? I had tried to make changes over the last few months myself.

I realized just how much work dominated my life. While my wife longed for the single life, I longed for more prestige at work. But I soon realized, after working myself like a dog, the extra money and pats on the back from the higher-ups meant nothing if I had no one to go home to.

This was the right thing to do. I needed to be home again. And I promised myself I wouldn't take my wife and our marriage for granted like I had before. I couldn't believe I once was glad April was around to keep Keisha busy so I could work more.

"If you'll take me back," I mumbled, still trying to work out what I'd say. But when I looked up, Keisha was standing right in front of me!

At first she didn't speak or move. She stood staring. The look on her face made me feel like she thought she'd seen a ghost. I didn't know what to say or do, either.

She could've very well asked me to leave, but she didn't. Keisha blinked a few times, then swallowed, but otherwise she remained frozen.

"What?" she finally said.

I shook my head. I didn't know what she meant.

"If I took you back what?" she asked.

"Uh, I just want us to talk. I've been calling, trying to get in touch with you." I wasn't prepared for this.

"For what? You left me, remember?" she pointed out, more than asked.

I could tell she was trying to swallow back tears. She was right. I did walk out on her. I allowed bullshit to take over me and I left my wife.

"Keisha, I made a mistake. Plain and simple, I made a mistake," I said.

We were still standing between the dining room and the family room. Although we spoke, neither of us made a move. She looked good, and I was suddenly jealous. I had hoped my time away had left her crumbled. I wanted to know she hurt like me.

Her next words gave me hope. Keisha cast her eyes downward and said, "We all make mistakes, Dexter. Nobody's perfect. Not you, not me. The question now is, what are we going to do about it?"

"That's why I'm here." I looked toward the family room. "You mind if we sit, so we can talk?"

Finally, after that, she moved. She walked into the

family room and put several DVDs on the sofa next to her. I took that to mean I needed to sit someplace else and I did.

The music was still playing. She had the satellite radio on the TV.

"Are you happy the way things are right now?" I just had to know. When that old song "If Loving You Is Wrong" came on, I developed courage. It wasn't just the song, it was that and the fact that I knew what she had done.

"I'm not happy with the way things are, but I also know I can't go back to the way they were. I just can't do it. I'm a different person now," Keisha said.

"So different that you enjoy being without me?" I looked around. "You and April are back to the way you were before I came along, and that's what you want, right?"

Keisha shook her head, saying "no," and tears fell from her eyes. I didn't say anything as I listened to her soft sobs. I knew nothing about the burdens she carried. I could guess, but I didn't really know.

"I'm just so confused," she sobbed.

I went to her side and took her into my arms. I could feel her body relax in my embrace and that made me feel good.

"What are you confused about? I love you, Keisha, and I always will," I assured her.

"No, I'm not worthy of your love. I'm not. I'm just like everyone said. They all tried to warn you about me, and they were right. I'm just not worthy."

My heart sank at her confession because in all the years we had been together I knew she fought to prove them all wrong. It was a battle I was proud to see her winning. Now she was giving up, giving in to the picture they all had painted.

"Keisha, they were not right about you. This whole thing, it was my fault too. I walked out. I left my home over bullshit. I felt embarrassed. Mama paid someone to dig up dirt on you and I felt like a fool. I should've at least heard you out, but I didn't. Come to find out, all that crap was about some other woman named Keisha Smith. She was ten years younger than you!" I shook my head, feeling embarrassed again. "The point I'm making is, I've allowed too many people to dictate how our lives should be, and for that I was wrong." I raised her chin with my fingers. "I want you to know, I've talked to Mama and Janet, and I told them without a doubt, if you agreed to take me back, I would not stand for their blatant disrespect any more!" I kissed her forehead. "And I mean it with all my heart. Our time apart has shown me that I was essentially as guilty as the rest of them. No, I didn't think you'd run around on me like you did, but because I basically allowed Mama and Janet to bring it up by talking about you, it was like I agreed with what they were saying." I stopped for a second while she used her hands to wipe her eyes. "And trust me, this isn't easy for me, either. I'm here, but there are a few things I know I need to work on," I somberly said.

Keisha

I realized how I responded to Dexter would determine the direction in which our marriage would go, but still I couldn't resist. I was no longer determined to prove him wrong. I just sat and allowed him to talk about what we would need to do to make the marriage work.

I wanted the security of our marriage, but I also wanted Melvin's spontaneity. As Dexter spoke, I started wondering just what Melvin was doing. He had wanted to be with me, but I told myself it was time for some soul searching. Suddenly I started regretting the fact that I chose to stay home.

If I had gone with Melvin, Dexter and I wouldn't be having the conversation and, essentially, I'd still be free.

"So I figured we'd go to counseling. It's really the only way we can try to make things work. I don't think we have a choice," Dexter was saying.

But maybe I did have a choice. What if I left Dexter for Melvin? I had asked myself that question quite a few times.

But the answer was always the same. If I were to move

in with Melvin, became his woman around the clock, I knew for certain things would change. He would turn into what I already had. I knew that if I chose Melvin over Dexter, soon Melvin would get comfortable like Dexter had. Then what? I'd be out there again looking for the next best thing.

Then I remembered what Melvin had offered. The sudden surge of joy that overcame me was shameful. Here my husband was spilling out his heart and his plan for our reconciliation and all I could do was think about just how long I'd have to wait before I could go to Melvin again.

"Yes, I'll go," I said.

The confusion on his face told me he must've moved on to an entirely new subject. But I wanted to make it clear.

"Yeah, I'll go to counseling. I think that's what we should do." While my lips spewed those words, my heart rested calmly because even as I sat there staring into the face of the man I truly loved, my mind couldn't stop thinking about the man who really made me feel excited about being loved.

Dexter

My biggest reward came two weeks after Labor Day. I knew getting back with my wife was the best thing to do, and we were set for our first counseling appointment October 3rd. I felt good knowing she had agreed to counseling. That told me we still had a fighting chance.

I wanted a sooner date, but that was the earliest Dr. Davidson could see us. In the meantime, April was less of a fixture in our home. I was prepared to pay for an apartment for her, but she was hardly ever around for me to even make the offer.

April and Keisha had been whispering in the kitchen and I did my best to act busy in our bedroom. I wanted to give them time to talk. I couldn't hear what they were talking about, but I was trying to remain positive. Ever since Keisha and I reunited, she and April seemed to have grown apart.

Don't get me wrong, they still spent lots of time talking on the phone, and they probably got together twice a week for dinner or drinks, and maybe every other weekend they went out on Friday or Saturday night, but it wasn't where it used to be and for that I was glad.

I was especially glad about the fact that they were no longer a mainstay at the clubs. Keisha told me they were trying new restaurants, going to movies, or parties for home interior, jewelry, and knockoff bags.

Either way, Keisha and I were settling into our old lives again and it felt good. When I say "our old lives," I don't mean the humdrum she once complained about. I even tried to stay off the couch while she was home. I'd save that for those moments when she was gone with April.

"So when are you leaving?" I heard Keisha ask as I walked into the kitchen.

"Well, I wanted to see when would be a good time to come get my things," April said.

I couldn't remember a time I had seen her look so mature. She was wearing a pair of slacks and a nice blouse.

"Hey, Dexter," she greeted me.

"Good to see you, April. You haven't been around much lately," I said. Keisha turned away from me as I spoke to April.

"Yeah, actually that's what we were talking about. Seems I'm finally getting out of your hair." She looked toward Keisha's back. "I'm moving, probably this weekend sometime," April said proudly.

I looked at Keisha, who still had her back to us.

"Oh really?" I didn't want to come off too happy about the news, but inside a parade was going on.

"Yep, met someone new and we've decided to live together. You know, to see how it would work," April said.

"Honey, why didn't you tell me about April and her new man? We should have you guys over for dinner sometime," I offered.

"Emm, yeah. We'll have to do that. But Robert is very busy, so we'll see."

"Okay." I shrugged and walked out of the kitchen. When I returned to grab my drink I'd left on the counter, it looked as if Keisha had been crying. She must've been sad about her friend leaving again. I figured we'd talk about it later.

"This makes no sense," I heard April whisper.

Keisha didn't say anything, but I agreed with April. It wasn't like the girl was about to vanish again for another five years. I really didn't see what Keisha was all choked up about. But knowing how emotional women could be, I didn't want to run the risk of saying anything. I especially didn't want them to think I was trying to listen in on their conversation.

Later, I heard a horn beep softly outside, but thought it was a neighbor being polite. Suddenly April ran from downstairs with a bag and said, "Later, you guys," as she slammed the front door shut.

"Oh, was that her new man? How come he didn't come in? I mean, I've never even met the man who is making my life a whole lot easier," I said jokingly.

Keisha looked up at me like I had just insulted her mother.

"Is everything okay?" I asked, trying to remove some of the obvious joy from my voice.

"Yeah, I'm good. Why?"

"Well, it seems lately like you've been a little down." I figured it was April's decision to leave, but I didn't want to take anything for granted.

"Well, I just want April to be happy, that's all. It's not going to be the same around here without her," Keisha admitted.

That's what I was banking on. But again, I didn't want

to break out and start laughing. Although I was happy she was leaving.

"You guys will still be able to see each other, it's not like she's leaving the state again, Keisha. Besides, this may be April's chance at something more substantial. Like what we have."

Keisha didn't respond. When she looked at me, her eyes seemed so far away. I hoped we'd make it to counseling before it was too late.

Keisha

I felt captive in my own body. It was a constant battle brewing between good and evil and I had no idea how to control it.

The more I told myself what I was doing was wrong, the less it seemed to matter. I was sad about April's leaving, but only because I had plans to hook up with Melvin later and she was going to be my way out of the house.

She told me Robert had a change in schedule and needed to come get her sooner than we expected. For the past few weeks, April had been my alibi. I'd pretend to go to dinner or a movie with her only to meet up with Melvin instead.

With April gone now, she was less likely to keep up with our well-rehearsed excuses I would spend time drilling her on. Now, I'd have to struggle to catch up with her and hope to God she wouldn't slip up and call the house while I was supposed to be out with her. But I figured I'd just have to take my chances.

* * *

When I was with Melvin, I was transported to another world completely. He didn't behave like we were doing anything wrong. He didn't make me feel guilty about stepping out on my husband. He just made me feel good. It was like my satisfaction was his only mission.

After school, I couldn't wait to get over to his place. A few times I'd sit there alone on his terrace, sipping tea instead of wine. I didn't want to do anything to tip Dexter off.

Melvin was far too accommodating. If I said we'd see each other Thursday evening but something came up, he always understood. One time I was on my way over to him, but wanted to stop home and change. When I saw Dexter on the couch, my heart sank.

I didn't even get the chance to call Melvin and say plans had changed. The next day when I called from school, he said he knew something had gone wrong, and asked if I could get away later. That was it, no worries, and no complaints about leaving him hanging.

Things had been going good with Dexter, but no matter how much he tried, he just wasn't Melvin.

Dexter kept talking about our upcoming counseling session like things were going to miraculously change with a doctor's help. As he spoke, I'd think of when I'd be able to get back to Melvin.

I was having a full-blown affair and I didn't even care. I didn't want to leave my husband, but I couldn't pull myself away from Melvin, either. I was weak. I didn't even care if Dexter stayed on the couch. I just wanted to be free to go to Melvin.

The last time he and I were together, he caught me gazing off.

"Let me fix it," he suddenly said.

"Huh?"

"Something's on your mind. It's not me, so I know it's not good. Let me fix it for you." He was so sincere.

I just stared at him. How could he fix what I kept telling myself was not broken?

"I'm fine. I am, really," I lied.

"Your mind is a million miles away." Melvin started unbuttoning my crisp white shirt. "Let me give you a good rubdown. Maybe that'll help."

And it did. His hands helped me relax so much that I was instantly turned on. He couldn't finish the massage good before I was begging him to put out the fire that burned so deep in me.

It was so intense when he flipped me onto my hands and knees and mounted me. His strong strokes were painstakingly accurate. Melvin's magic hips would dip and rotate, sending his wand deeper and deeper into my sweet pot like he was stirring up something good. His motions hit and massaged my spot just the way I liked. I came so hard, it felt like a vein was about to burst in my head. I was sure this was what an aneurysm would be like.

After that mind-blowing experience, he just eased down and sucked the nectar from my throbbing clit with the gentle softness you'd use on a newborn. When my body started twitching again, he quickly entered me and didn't move.

"Wwwhat's wrong?" I managed after finding my words.

"Nothing . . . eeemmm nothing at all, I just want to feel you coming on me, this feeling keeps me awake at nights. I just want to please you," he said right before my eyes rolled back up into my head. I didn't think it possible to come any harder than I had before.

That day I was determined to suck the color off

Melvin's dick. After he came, he helped me into the shower, washed me, then sucked me off again. It was like the earth moved when we were one. And Melvin would keep pleasing me until I'd literally beg him to stop.

When it was all over, he sent me home to my husband.

Later, I sat on the sofa picking at my nails. I didn't want to look at the clock because that might indicate I wanted to be some place else.

"Oh, I almost forgot to tell you," Dexter started. "Mama and Janet invited us to dinner tomorrow night."

I looked at him. Things had also improved where his mother and sister were concerned, but I didn't feel they were good enough for me to want to sit and eat with them.

He must've sensed what I was thinking, because he reached out to me. I looked at his outstretched arms and reluctantly went.

"I know it's not going to be easy to forgive them. I've allowed them to get away with hurting you for far too long, but we've gotta try to meet them halfway. They're trying, Keisha, so we have to try, too."

I kept thinking about whether I really was stuck for the night. I had no interest in going to dinner with my mother- and sister-in-law, but I wondered if I could make Dexter think otherwise.

"Have you talked with them since we got back together?" I wanted to know.

"Of course, I just told you they invited us to dinner. Why?"

"Well, I was just thinking that maybe you needed to spend some time with them before we agree to dinner."

When Dexter gave me a sideways glance, I thought I

had been figured out. I thought he'd realized I was just trying to get him out of the house.

Instead, he said, "You have every reason to be concerned. I'd feel the same way if I was you, but, trust me, Keisha. I have made it clear to them that they'd better treat you with the utmost respect. They're trying. What do you say you give them a chance?"

I looked into my husband's eyes and told myself for the umpteenth time that he was a good man. Still, despite his goodness, I wanted another. It was like I couldn't help myself. I was hooked on Melvin and I had long ago passed the point of no return. I wanted so badly to be with him whenever I wasn't. Being outside his presence was like torture.

"Okay, well, let me go to the store. I need to pick up a few things," I lied.

"The dinner is tomorrow, Keisha, besides you should know you don't need to worry about picking up anything." It was like he was fighting me.

"I know that, but if I'm going to your mother's house for dinner, there's no way in the world I'm going to walk in there empty-handed," I offered, hoping that would be enough.

"You want me to go with you?" he asked.

"No," I shook my head. "I won't be long," I assured him. I snatched up my keys and purse and ran out of the door. Once I pulled my car out of our subdivision, I realized my cell was still on the counter, but I didn't care. I'd have to improvise.

The minute I walked into HEB's grocery store, I went straight to the back, dropped a bunch of coins into a pay phone, and called Melvin.

Dexter

The three most important women in my life were finally calling a truce and I couldn't be happier. When we pulled up in front of Mama's house in River Oaks, Josephine, the maid, was just leaving.

Keisha and I waved good-bye as I parked the car. As we got out, I saw Keisha surveying the outside of the house. It was massive by anyone's standards. I wanted to help ease her anxiety, tell her things had changed, but I figured that would only make her more nervous. I only hoped Mama and Janet wouldn't prove me wrong.

This was not Keisha's first time at my Mom's, but it would be her first time since the new rules had been established. Mama and Janet had been warned that harrassing Keisha was off-limits.

We had been sitting in the dining room as Mama put the finishing touches on dinner. I looked around and my sister and my wife were finally getting along. The joy I felt was indescribable.

"So what did you do?" Keisha asked Janet.

"Well, I walked into the restroom, and this woman could see I was nervous. So she said, 'Ma'am are you okay?' I shook my head. I said, 'No, actually I'm not. I'm on the blind date from hell and I really need to get away from this man!'"

Keisha and Janet broke out in laughter together. "What did she say?" Keisha asked.

"The woman looked at me and said, 'Don't worry, I'll help.' So this stranger, Kim, made it her mission to help me get out of my fix and she did. She told me to go back out to the table and act like everything was fine. I did, and a few minutes later, she comes storming up to our table. 'Janet! My goodness! Here you are! We've been searching all over for you. It's your sister, she's been taken to the emergency room. I'm glad you wrote the address to the restaurant down or I don't know what we would've done.'"

Janet shook her head, replaying the scene, "'We've been trying your cell phone,' the woman said. Fred looked horrified. 'Oh, you need me to give you a ride?' he offered. But before I could respond, Kim turned to him and said, 'Sir, this is a family emergency; we've got it under control. My cousin and I are going to make sure she gets to the hospital. C'mon, Janet!' She all but pulled my arm and we rushed out of the restaurant." Janet eased back in the chair. "I never saw old Fred again and I was glad. Whew!"

Keisha giggled and I sat amazed.

"What about Kim?" Keisha asked.

"Oh, we're still friends. As a matter of fact, we're planning a shopping trip to San Marcos in a few weeks. You know, hit all of the outlets."

I was glad to see Keisha getting along with my sister. I had never even thought about Janet dating. I was so used to her and Mama being all up in my business, I never stopped to think about her even having a social life.

Mama appeared at the entryway. "Shall we move to the dining room?"

Dinner went better than expected. For the most part, the conversation was light. Mama pretty much behaved herself and Janet actually tried to engage Keisha in more small talk. I felt good. But I also knew the night couldn't come off picture perfect.

When Mama brought out her upside-down pineapple cake, I thought we were coasting through the evening pretty well. After slicing it, she looked at Keisha and asked, "So, are you looking forward to counseling?"

I tossed Mama a warning glare. She acknowledged me, but still charged forward. "I say if you need a doctor to fix your marriage, then maybe you don't need to be married," Mama said sweetly, with ease.

I held my breath and prepared for the worst as I observed Keisha. She said, "Well, Hattiemae, in this day and age what you had with your husband is rare. To have a successful marriage for nearly forty years! Wow, you could certainly teach us younger couples quite a bit."

First Mama's face contorted into what I thought was about to be the calm before the storm. I just knew she was about to explode and light into Keisha. I watched closely as her arched eyebrows elevated, and her mouth twisted up into a pout. But when she spoke, all she uttered was an almost inaudible "Emh hmmm."

And that was it. That's when I knew for sure things were gonna be just fine with the three most important women in my life.

Keisha

When I called to tell Melvin there had been a change in plans, once again he seemed to understand. He explained to me that business was taking him back to Philly and this time he'd be gone for two weeks.

I wondered what Melvin did while we were apart, but told myself I had no right to even ask. Once before when I asked how he could be satisfied with so little, as far as our relationship was concerned, he looked at me and said, "If having only a piece of you is all I can get, I'll make due, I'll make it work."

And that's exactly what he did. He made it work. Melvin planned everything around my schedule and me, whenever he could. I had no idea how I'd survive without him for two weeks straight and when I shared that with him in bed one Sunday afternoon, when I was supposed to be visiting a friend's church, he said, "If you're finding it too hard after the first week, fly to Philly and meet me. You can stay one night or two, however long you can get away and we'll see if that doesn't help."

I looked at him, amazed. With him it was always about

me. That's why I decided I'd never give up what we had. There was simply no way I could.

Dexter and I were set to begin counseling the following week. I was looking forward to it only because a part of me never believed that talking to someone could make another person behave differently.

Here it was—we hadn't even stepped foot in Dr. Davidson's office for a session, but I had already decided counseling wasn't going to work for me. I admitted to myself from the beginning, I was just going to keep Dexter happy.

On the way back home after dinner with his mom and sister, I kept trying to figure out a way to see Melvin before he left Saturday afternoon. Since I hadn't heard from April in a while, I figured a call to her might be just the thing to get me out of the house.

I dialed her new number and she answered on the first ring, "Hey April, you expecting a call or something?"

"Yeah, I'm waiting on Robert to call. Keisha, I'm so sorry I haven't been a good friend lately, but you know I'm trying my best to show Robert that I can be a good woman and—"

"So you want me to come over Saturday morning? No, we don't have anything planned. Okay, I'll see you then," I said, interrupting her tirade.

"Oh, are you trying to see Melvin or something? Dexter must be close."

"Yeah. Okay, I'll be there," I sang into the phone cheerfully.

"Why don't the four of us meet up for breakfast?" April offered.

"That sounds great. We can maybe do brunch afterwards. How's that?" I compromised.

"Cool."

I pushed the "end" button on the phone and looked over to see if my husband suspected anything.

"I was wondering what was up with you and April. Hadn't heard her name in a while," he said.

"Yeah, well we've been hooking up, but you know she's busy trying to get her life in order."

"Well, maybe once she gets settled we can have her and her new man over, or we can all go to dinner." Dexter turned into our subdivision.

I was thrilled that I'd get to see Melvin the next morning. I wanted nothing more than to go home, shower, go to sleep, and hurry tomorrow up.

But Dexter had other plans for me. When I got out of the shower, the entire house was dark. It wasn't until I saw him walking with a burning candle that I realized he was trying to be romantic. I smiled at him when he put it down and ran out of our bedroom.

I heard music a few minutes later. He returned wearing silk boxers and a smile. I didn't hesitate to make love to my husband, because I knew exactly what to expect. I even knew how to make it last or make it fast.

That night I chose fast, because the quicker he was done, the faster I could prepare for my Saturday morning rendezvous.

"I love you so much. . . . I've missed you," he sang. And at the moment when I needed it least, my heart began to sink. For a fleeting moment, I started wondering why this man couldn't be enough for me. But when I dipped down, when I took him into my mouth, and realized there were no feelings of sheer delight, I gave myself permission to want what I knew only Melvin could give.

Within minutes of his seduction, Dexter was begging

to enter me. But I was saving that for the sure thing. I knew the delay would give me the results I was after.

When I felt his hardness, his body tensed at my touch. Dexter stroked me with such power, I almost forgot I was with my husband. My mind had strayed to Melvin a while ago. I couldn't help but mentally make comparisons with every touch, kiss, and moan. Dexter begged me not to stop, as I rode his leg and tried to suck him dry. I did this while firmly massaging his balls and I knew this was blowing his mind. But while I loved him, my mind lusted for Melvin.

"Damn, Keisha!"

His voice brought me back to where I was. When his body jerked, I exhaled. He grabbed my head, held me tightly as he released a belly-wrenching moan. Moments later, I heard light snoring.

This time I didn't feel the least bit slighted because I knew my real joy would come in the morning.

Dexter

Anytime anyone complained about my wife again all I had to do was remember last night. I was so glad to be back at home, working on our marriage and witnessing change between her and my family.

Once April left our home it was like everything had fallen back into place. At first, I felt pressured to keep up this façade, but we were finally returning to normal and I was glad.

I decided to call Roger after work Saturday. I wanted to see what he and Larry were up to, but I should've known his player behind would be wrapped up with some woman. When he didn't answer by the third ring and his machine didn't pick up, I figured his Friday night date had rolled over to Saturday morning.

Times like these made me miss the friendship I used to share with the fellas, but honestly I just got so tired of hearing them talk about my wife, that, once we reunited, I started pulling back.

It was one thing to dislike someone, but disrespecting another man's wife? Well, that was going way too far.

I figured I'd call Larry and see what he was up to. When he answered, I regretted calling him in the first place.

"Yo, man, I heard you went back to that wife of yours," he said.

"Yeah, Larry, Keisha and I are back together and things are better than they've ever been."

"Hmmm," was all he said.

It didn't take long for me to grow bored with our conversation, so I let him go. My next call was to Mama and Janet. I thought it strange that Mama asked if I had seen my sister. I wondered why I would've seen Janet early on a Saturday morning, but Mama told me Janet mentioned inviting Keisha to the outlet malls with her and Kim.

I was glad to hear that, although I knew Keisha was out garage-sale shopping with April.

Once my calls had been made, I decided I'd get up and cut the grass in both the front and back yard. I also decided to throw a few steaks on the grill to show Keisha how much I appreciated our romantic evening last night.

When Keisha walked in hours later and walked straight to our bedroom, I noticed she didn't have any bags from the garage sale. I assumed her shopping hadn't been successful.

A few minutes later, I went into our bedroom to see what she was doing. I could've sworn she jumped when she heard me.

"Hey, couldn't find anything at the garage sale?" I asked.

For a moment she didn't answer, she had a faraway expression across her face. "Keisha? Are you okay? I asked about the garage sale," I said.

"Oh, it was a waste of our time. We went around to several but didn't find anything. Finally we gave up and went to eat."

"You didn't find anything you liked?" I found that hard to believe.

"Nope. After a while I became frustrated. I'm really kind of tired. It was hot out there. I just want to take a shower and take a nap. You'll call me when dinner is ready?" she asked.

"Sure, you go ahead. I'll finish grilling and I'll wake you when everything is ready. You want anything before you take a shower?"

She shook her head, saying "no," and I left her at the edge of the bed. I felt a little better when I heard the water running.

Once we finished dinner, I cleaned the mess I had made in the kitchen and hung around to see if my wife wanted to do anything.

Keisha said she was looking forward to a night of reading. There were a few good books she wanted to catch up on, so I told her if she changed her mind, just let me know.

Sadly, a part of me was happy she didn't want to go out or do anything. After dinner I was looking forward to stretching out on the sofa and finding a good game to watch.

It dawned on me then that I needed to remind her about counseling. I sure hoped Dr. Davidson could help us.

Honestly, I was hoping he would tell Keisha that she needed to realize what she had at home and know there was nothing better in those streets. But it looked as if she had already figured that out on her own.

I briefly considered canceling our appointment altogether, but I decided we definitely needed to go.

I was certain once the doctor told her a good wife stayed at home with her husband, I knew we would be able to wrap up the counseling sessions.

Keisha

Saturday morning couldn't come fast enough for me. I must've been dressed and out of the house before eight in the morning. While Dexter tried to linger in bed like he wanted to sleep in, I was up and in the shower.

He looked up and said, "It's too early, come back to bed."

"I'm meeting April this morning. We want to hit a few garage sales in the Memorial area. You know if we're not early, all the good stuff will be gone."

He pouted. But I was trying not to be sidetracked. I was on a serious mission. He got what he wanted the night before. I had done my wifely duty. Now it was my turn to get some real satisfaction. I rushed out before he could protest any further.

I jumped into my car and raced down the street. I nearly ran two red lights before stopping at another and warning myself to calm down. I didn't even call to tell Melvin I was on my way. But I knew I didn't need to, either.

I parked across the street from his building in the paid lot and speed-walked up to the elevator. When a car didn't come fast enough, I punched the button a couple more times.

"They're running slow this morning ma'am, but they'll be down soon," said the doorman. I was embarrassed, but then I told myself if he knew what I was rushing to, he'd understand my impatience.

When I finally stepped off the elevator, I used my key to let myself into Melvin's place. I removed the top to my warm-ups at the door. I slipped out of my tennis shoes and walked to the stairs.

By the time I got up the stairs, I could hear his soft snoring from the bedroom's entrance. I stepped out of my pants and walked over to his bed.

I climbed in right next to his warm body and inhaled deeply. Oh, how I missed his scent. At my touch, he rolled over and pulled me close to him.

"What took you so long, I was just dreaming about you," he whispered in my ear.

"Well, I guess your dream came true, baby. I'm here now."

Without opening his eyes, he started rubbing my shoulders. His fingers felt so good. It amazed me how this man could love me like he'd known me for years. He knew exactly which spots to hit, and where to touch me. At first, I was a bit disappointed, thinking I wouldn't get adequate attention because he was half-asleep.

But Melvin quickly rose to the occasion. He went down first, I knew to ensure I'd start off with an orgasm. When he was done, he came back up, bent his knees and lifted my midsection. When he entered me, he was hard as steel. He filled me so much that I felt him despite my overflowing wetness. In the throes of passion, he looked deep into my eyes and asked, "How many do you need?"

"W-what, babe?" I lifted my head ever so slightly.

"I need to know how many orgasms you need to hold you over until Friday," he said.

Two hours later, we lay in bed completely spent but satisfied.

"What time does your flight leave?" I asked.

"Not until four-thirty this afternoon. Don't worry, we've got time for rounds two and three," he said.

"Oh, I told April we'd meet her and Robert for brunch," I said, suddenly mad at myself for not thinking.

"It's okay. I spoke to him last night and told him we had to take a rain check."

I looked at him. "How did you know to do that?"

"Keisha, we haven't seen each other in days. I figured you were using April as a way to see me before I left. I know you don't *need* to eat with her and Robert. Baby, I got everything you need right here," he insisted so sincerely.

"Well, why don't you give it to me then?" I laughed.

Our time together made me feel like everything was sure to be okay. It was funny to me how satisfaction had a way of making everything better. That was the case with me. I could tolerate my husband and what had once again become our humdrum life because I was more satisfied than ever before.

After a while it didn't matter to me that I had to rely on someone else for that satisfaction.

Back at home that Saturday night, I kept thinking about the following Friday. That's when I'd see Melvin again. I hadn't told Dexter about my plans to go to Philly just yet. I was waiting on the right time.

As he lay stretched across the sofa, I figured there was no sense in putting off the inevitable.

"Hey hon, I need to go to DC next Friday. I'll be back Saturday afternoon," I tossed in before he could protest. Melvin had already bought the ticket, so if he had to, we'd change my flight to Saturday instead of Sunday.

"Oh, I wish you had said something sooner. There

was a weekend seminar for work that I backed out of because I didn't want to leave you alone." Dexter sounded truly disappointed.

"Well, check into it Monday. I mean, my trip is supposed to be two days, but I wasn't sure how you'd feel about me being gone, so I told the district I could try and cram everything in a day and a half."

"As long as you're not going with April, I don't care. No offense, but you and April traveling is never a good idea, especially after what happened with Aruba."

I was glad we could laugh about it now, but the truth was if he knew where I was really going he'd probably wish I were running off with April. I also made a mental note to call her, and start coaching her so she wouldn't blow my cover.

By midweek, I had a serious pep in my step because Dexter was able to do the weekend seminar for work and I was off to la-la land.

Earlier, I had told Melvin that he might need to switch my flight to return Saturday. I was glad that would no longer be the case.

"Don't forget, counseling starts Monday," Dexter reminded me, breaking my train of thought. I suffered a moment of panic. I wondered if counseling could be somewhat brainwashing as well. I dreaded the thought that there could possibly be words out there strong enough to make me get off that new high I'd discovered, so counseling put a sense of fear in me.

That was even more of a reason I felt I needed a weekend away with Melvin. It was like my days of happiness were numbered, so I wanted to do what I could to make the very best of what little free time I had left.

Dexter

"We need you to work a double," my boss's voice boomed at my office door.

"No can do, Bob," I said quickly, getting up from my desk. I had really been trying to cut back on the hours at work. My plans were to go home and get ready to take Keisha out for a nice dinner.

I remember that day so well, not only because it marked one of just a few times I had refused to work overtime, but for another reason as well.

That was the day I found out about my wife's affair, and it had to be the worst day of my entire life. Sure, I had suspected and even forgiven what I thought were minor indiscretions. But to be able to put a name and face to the actual person, well, that hurt beyond words. I know I had an indiscretion of my own . . . . but the dates on the pictures proved what I had done was a drop in the bucket compared to this extramarital relationship my wife was involved in.

Looking back at it now, I guess she was too much for me, because for months she had been carrying on with some man named Melvin Johnson. He worked in

commercial real estate and, thanks to Mama, not only did
I have pictures to prove they'd been together, but a complete outline of the man's life in black and white.

He owned a loft in downtown Houston and there
were enough pictures to prove my wife had been to his
place regularly. There were even pictures of the two on
his balcony. Those pictures were kind of blurry, like
they'd been taken from a great distance. But I didn't
need a close-up to see him between her legs as he had
her pinned against the railing of his balcony for the
whole world to see.

Mama, or the person she hired, left no stone un-
turned. It turned out that trip to DC? Well, it was really
a trip to the Hilton hotel and the airport in Philly.
There, they were a little risky. There were pictures of
them on the dance floor, even pictures of them all over
each other before they could make it into room 2834.
The woman in the pictures was not my wife—not the
way she was carrying on like she had no responsibilities
or commitments elsewhere. I couldn't believe it, even
though the proof was right there.

According to what I was reading, they spent hours in
the hotel room in Philly ordering room service. I was
beyond devastated.

We had already had the appointment to see Dr.
Davidson. And here she was making a fool out of me all
over again. I wasn't sure how I would handle the information I had, but I knew things were definitely about to
get worse before they got better with us.

My problem was, I still loved Keisha. People often
said I was the best thing to happen to her, but it was
truly the other way around. I loved my wife so much,
sometimes I would dream of her leaving me for another

man and I'd wake up and stare at her until the sun came up.

I knew then it was stupid for me to want to fight for my marriage, but I felt myself losing out to anger. I knew one thing for sure. This time, I wouldn't be the one to leave my house again.

I decided to take a few days off from work. I needed to gather my thoughts and figure out my next course of action.

Mama had the package delivered to me at work. I was walking out to lunch when Penny stopped me. Our relationship had never fully recovered from her failed seduction attempt.

Sometimes, we'd be on a first-name basis, others I wasn't sure if we were even on speaking terms. I usually waited for her to take my cue.

"Oh, Mr. Saintjohn, I thought you were out, this came for you a little while ago." She handed me the large envelope. I started to leave it for when I came back, but ripped it open and nearly lost the strength in my legs when a picture of my half-naked wife fell to the floor.

"Dexter, uh, I mean, Mr. Saintjohn?" I heard her voice laced with true concern.

I reached down for the picture. "Um, ah, yeah, I'm good. Ah, just hold all of my calls will you?"

"But I thought you were headed to lunch," I heard her say as I ran back to my office. I sat locked in there for hours, mulling over the tons and tons of pictures and information.

Once I had seen everything at least twice, I immediately called my supervisor and took emergency leave. I was sick beyond words.

How could I have been so wrong about her? I thought we were on the road to recovery. In consultation,

Dr. Davidson had even told us he had seen couples worse off than us and was confident we'd be just fine. Instead, my world was shattered. Keisha was still at school when I got home.

I looked around the house. Where had I gone wrong, I wondered? I had changed my behavior just like Dr. Davidson suggested. I still relaxed on the couch, but I rarely did it when Keisha was home.

She had told the counselor seeing me like that made her feel uninspired. She said I'd stretch out on the couch and she'd immediately feel like we were old.

Keisha admitted that she wished I could be more like the men she read about in romance novels. I remembered when he asked us to describe our idea of a romantic evening. Unfortunately, I was looking at pictures that told me she had already lived it out with another man.

I looked at him, the complete opposite of me. I was brown-skinned, with a thick body. He looked slim, light, with a goatee.

Why couldn't he find his own woman? He didn't look bad. From the pictures, it looked like he had some money, so why couldn't he get any woman he wanted?

The phone rang. I didn't have to look at the caller ID to tell it was gonna be Mama.

"Yeah," I said, trying to swallow back some of my anger.

"Are you okay?" she asked.

"What do you think?" I asked. When she didn't answer, I said, "Are you happy? You were able to prove that my wife is having an affair. Are you happy, Mama?" I screamed.

"Baby, I'm just looking out for you. You deserve so much more. If she doesn't know how good she has it—"

"I didn't ask for your help! I was working on my marriage, Mama. I told you to stay out of it."

"Dexter Charles Saintjohn, I raised you better than this. Why would you sit there and be somebody's fool?" Mama asked.

"I'm nobody's fool! Just because I love my wife? So that makes me a fool, huh? Why can't you understand? I love her, Mama!"

"But look what she's doing to you. She has no respect for the institution of marriage. You deserve so much better," Mama insisted.

"I don't want anybody but Keisha. She's my wife. I love her and I need you to back off!"

"What are you saying, Dexter?"

"I'm saying I want you to stay out of my life! I'm through with you. This was the last straw!" I screamed. I knew my anger was misdirected, but I was boiling, and she was near.

"Dexter, are you telling me you are going to stay with this jezebel? If that's the case, I must warn you, I will remove you from my will."

I just hung up. I was beyond frustrated and far beyond tears. I knew the truth: Keisha was my absolute everything and my life wasn't right without her. I had already tried to be without her and I was miserable, but the pictures staring back at me told a different story on her part.

It was obvious she didn't care about our marriage or me. My heart told me to hang in there, to fight for my wife, but Keisha was making it hard. I knew what I was going to do, but first I was determined to talk to this Melvin Johnson face-to-face, man-to-man.

Then, after that, I'd deal with my wife. I was finally tired of being played for a fool.

Keisha

If I had the slightest inkling of what was waiting for me the moment I arrived from the airport, I would've turned my tail around, gone straight back to Memphis, and crawled back beneath Melvin. This had been our second getaway weekend, and it had gone off close to perfectly, so I had no need to worry, or so I thought.

But how could I have known? On the plane I was busy trying to correct papers and preparing myself mentally for the week I'd have to endure before I could see Melvin again.

That's what life had become, useless time between my fixes. Still, I was determined to go through the motions of making my marriage work. I just needed to be truly sure about what I wanted before I made any drastic moves. I had arranged for April to use Robert's car to pick me up and take me home. I figured we could catch up on each other's lives, since we really hadn't seen one another in quite a while.

I also had to make sure she understood she was still my alibi and that she was not to ever call the house unless she first tried my cell phone.

Our system had been working pretty well, but I also knew it wouldn't take long for April to get thrown off and slip up.

"So, how are things with your men?" she asked with all seriousness, the moment I tossed my bag into her backseat.

"I'm trying my best to keep them both happy," I answered honestly.

"Well, things are going much better than I expected with Robert, oops," she said as she ran a red light the minute we got off I-10 on Fry Road.

I really didn't want to hear about her and Robert. I only wanted to think or talk about Melvin. I wanted to share with her just how much he had done for me. Selfish, I know, but that, too, unfortunately, is what I had been reduced to. Melvin really made me believe it was all about me.

But April was so caught up in being the perfect little woman for Robert, I didn't want to disrupt what she had going.

By the time we pulled up at my house, I was ready for her to go. She insisted on helping me in with my bags. When we walked into the house, the very first thing we saw was a large black and white picture of me spread across Melvin's terrace. I didn't have to explain what his head was doing between my legs, because the smile plastered on my face made it all too obvious.

"Ohmygod!" April screamed.

I dropped my bag, prepared to snatch the picture down from a string where it dangled. But there were plenty more, hanging from our banister. On the floor in the formal living room, pictures were scattered all over, each one displaying several stages of my time with Melvin.

"What the hell?" I was alarmed at the invasion of my

privacy. But then it suddenly dawned on me, if these pictures were all over our house, it was because my *husband* had put them there.

It was strange; a sudden calm came over me before sheer panic settled in. I turned to April and said, "I think you should leave."

She looked up at me, unsure. Before she could say anything, Dexter appeared in the doorway. He looked beyond me and directly at April.

"So you knew about this?" he asked. There was a scary type of rage reflected in his eyes. His eyes were red, nearly swollen. He had either been crying or seething with anger for hours.

April looked at me, then at him. She didn't even need to answer, because guilt was all over her face.

"You knew? It's all your fucking fault. I searched for you, brought you back into our lives and this is how you betray me, my home, my generosity?" I put my hands up trying to calm Dexter.

"I, ah, I didn't do anything," April cried.

"Just go!" I screamed at April.

"No, don't leave, you stay right here!" he demanded.

"Leave now, April. I'll call you later."

April quickly shuffled out of the door. I turned and looked at Dexter. "You should calm down," I said.

He stepped toward me. I could smell the strong scent of tequila. I knew I was in major trouble if he had turned to tequila.

"I believed in you. I trusted you, and this is how you repay me?" he waved his arms about. Pictures were everywhere. "I loved you. I only tried to give you the best. I may have worked too much, but it was all for you."

Dexter screamed.

"Don't fool yourself. You worked for you." I was afraid and relieved at the same time. A part of me knew no matter how this ended, I had someplace to go, someplace else where I was definitely wanted. Funny how that thought was enough to give me courage.

"You wanted to prove to all of those people that you were better than the next man. You neglected home. I begged you to pay half the attention to home as you did to work, but you wouldn't." I knew I was wrong to make this a work issue. It was far from that. The truth was I had just gotten caught up. And while there was a sliver of guilt in me, because I did feel bad, even the guilty will turn defensive when under attack, and I was no different.

I decided not to make this any more difficult than it needed to be. I still had Melvin's key and could go crash at his place if I needed to.

"You sat in front of Dr. Davidson and said you were committed, but all the while you had no intention of working things out. You made a fool out of me," he yelled. The anger in his face and voice scared me, but for some reason, I refused to back down.

"That's not true. I agreed to counseling because I wanted to try and make things work. But think about it, Dexter, you wasted no time returning to the same uninspired workaholic you were before you left. You tried to say things would be different, but they weren't. Yeah, for the first few weeks, it even looked like you'd try to change, try to act interested in me and my life, but it didn't take long for you to return to your old ways."

Dexter looked at me and said, "We made a promise before God and everyone we know. How could you go back on your word, your promise to me? Our vows . . .

Don't you even feel the slightest bit of remorse? You cold-hearted bit . . ." he pulled back.

But the hatred I saw in his eyes made me cringe even more. I wanted to touch my chest, to try and calm my heart because of how fast it was beating, but I was afraid to move.

Suddenly Dexter turned and stormed out of the room. A few minutes later, I heard drawers slamming and a crashing noise.

I rushed back to our bedroom and stopped suddenly when I found him standing in the middle of a pile of clothes, shoes, and other things—my things!

"Oh! Don't even tell me, you're leaving me again," I hissed.

He looked up at me briefly, then through gritted teeth said, "No, you're the one leaving this time."

Dexter

I only wanted to let Keisha know that I knew what she had done. I didn't mean to go off on April, but I still felt like she was partly to blame. My wife wasn't thinking about cheating before April reappeared, I just knew it.

I wanted Keisha to act like she was sorry, and when she didn't, I nearly lost my mind. I started throwing her stuff into bags, suitcases, and everything else I could think of. When I told her she was leaving, she crossed her arms and stood staring at me. She wouldn't budge.

"Where the hell am I supposed to go?" she asked, defiantly.

"I don't give a damn where you go, you just need to leave here!"

We were in a house divided. She refused to leave and I refused to act like all was well.

After some soul-searching, I found some truth in quite a bit of what she said. It hurt, but I knew I was partially to blame for her affair. I had driven her into the arms of another man. And the way I was going on, it was as if my betrayal didn't exist. I know it was a double standard, but I knew I'd take that to the grave.

The Monday after I confronted her, I called Dr. Davidson the minute she left for work. I explained to him that I had found out—and Keisha had admitted—that she'd been having an affair all along.

He signed us up for an emergency session, but she refused to go. When she arrived home about a week after we had agreed to the new separate living arrangements—Keisha on the first floor, me in our master bedroom—she called me into the kitchen.

Keisha stood on one side of the island. I was on the other. She had been crying.

"Dexter, what's been going on between us is weighing heavily on me. You could do so much better than me."

"Is this your way of saying you want out of this marriage?" I asked straightforwardly. I was so tired of being Mr. Nice Guy.

"I don't know," she answered.

"Do you love him?"

She shook her head.

"What about me? Do you still love me?" I asked. I was so afraid of the answer, but I had to know.

"I do, but I'm not sure if I'm in love with you," she said sadly.

"Because of him? How could you just allow yourself to be led astray? First by April, then by this man? What does he have that I don't?" I needed to know.

"It's nothing like that. He's just . . . He wants to know what my day was like. He cares about how I'm handling this thing with you. He is genuinely interested in me. He um, he compliments me, makes me feel like a woman," she continued. Her eyes shot downward. "He makes me feel wanted, like I'm still desirable."

She couldn't tell how much her words were hurting me. But with everything she claimed she got from him, without her saying it, I knew she turned to him because it wasn't available from me.

I couldn't remember the last time I asked her what happened at school. The last time I told her how good she looked must've been at our anniversary celebration. The last time we had sex, I fell asleep afterward and woke the next morning to find her dressed and on her way out the door. I wondered now if she was rushing off to be with him, again to get what I didn't give.

Looking at her suffering and knowing how I felt, I again wished Mama would've stayed out of my business. I wouldn't be able to care that my wife was cheating if I didn't know about it.

Why couldn't she have been more careful? I wanted what we had. I wanted our love to go back to the days before April and Melvin.

"So you were planning to leave me for him?" I asked her.

"That's what you don't understand. I don't have to," she cried.

"What's that supposed to mean?" I asked, feeling the anger building again.

"He is all about me. He wants what I want. If I want you, he just wants me to give him whatever I can."

"What kind of man is that? He's with another man's wife and he doesn't care if you stay? He cares nothing about you, Keisha. You deserve more. You deserve a man who cares about your well-being, who provides for you. Hell, you deserve your husband! You have all of that in me, in case you haven't noticed." After a long silence, I said, "You know what, Keisha, go to him. Enough is enough. I'm tired."

Keisha

I wanted to run to Melvin and tell him we'd been found out. I wondered what would happen to what we had. The sheer thought made me feel a loneliness that ached to my core.

It dawned on me that I had cheated before, but I had never experienced anything like this. A small part of me knew if I left Dexter, with time, Melvin might turn on me. I was determined not to leave my husband for him because I knew the inevitable would happen. But what I should've been doing is thinking about what was soon to come my way.

When the words fell from my husband's lips, I nearly stumbled back. "Did you just tell me to go?" I asked with amazement.

"I'm tired, Keisha. It's obvious he does things for you that I can't possibly do, so why sit here and suffer? Go to him!"

Those words stayed with me as I made my way up to Melvin's front door. I couldn't find my key, but I didn't [ ]to. The screaming voices I heard made me [ ]was even in the right building.

Before I could do anything, the door flew open and an attractive brown-skinned woman in a flight attendant's uniform looked me up and down.

"Yes?" She looked to the bags at my feet. She didn't try to hide her attitude, flipping her hand to her hip.

"Um. I ah . . ."

"Can I help you?" she snapped, her words laced with attitude.

I swallowed back tears. I wanted to ask who she was, and why she was in Melvin's house, screaming, no less. But I really wanted this all to be a nightmare. I needed to ask her where Melvin was, but I just couldn't find my voice. I shook my head slowly and was about to turn and leave, but that's when I heard Melvin's voice.

"Paige, who's there?" He suddenly appeared at the door wearing a wedding band I had never seen before.

"Oh, Keisha . . ." his voice trailed off. It wasn't a surprised tone or even one conveying shock. It was just like, "oh."

Paige looked at me, then at Melvin. "What is going on here? Is this that woman *he* was talking about? First her husband and now she shows up with bags at her feet?" Paige shook her head, making her rumpled ponytail move about her head. She threw her hands up. "I don't need this kind of crap. You best start talking, Melvin," she hissed.

"I'll handle this," Melvin said, all but pushing Paige to the side and stepping completely into the hall. He quickly closed the door behind him.

"Melvin, what is going on here?"

I watched his Adam's apple bounce when he swallowed and looked at me with sad eyes. "Um, my wife, Paige, she's my wife," he pinched the bridge of his nose and closed his eyes.

Oh, the horror!

"Your w-what? You mean I left my husband for you and you're already married? How could you not tell me something like this?" I felt like such an idiot.

"Wait, it's not what you think, Keisha. Paige and I are, well, we were separated. But she came back and wants to work it out." He looked down. "I only considered it because of Dexter. He came to see me," he admitted.

I couldn't believe my ears. I had so many questions, but I didn't have the slightest desire to even start asking. I closed my eyes just as the tears seeped out. "What have I done?" I leaned against the wall, defeated.

"You can still stay here. Let's just talk about this. I mean, Paige and I just reconciled," he said. "You just say the word, Keisha. I mean it."

When his door swung open again, I was glad I had moved away from it. Paige jumped on him and started clawing his face and chest.

"Just say the word!" she screamed. "You never said you started seeing someone else. You bastard! I can't believe I even considered taking you back."

I grabbed my bags and left them fighting on the floor.

In the elevator, I started going over my options. I couldn't believe what my life had been reduced to. I know this was stupid, but hours later, as I sat in my hotel room, I dialed the number to my old house.

When Dexter heard my voice, there was silence, then I heard the dial tone.

"Oh God, what have I done?"

Dexter

Just the thought of her trying to contact me made me mad all over again. I started thinking back to the man who helped her ruin my marriage. I knew this call would come, once she showed up at his place. A part of me didn't want to believe she had gone to him, but she had.

When I finally faced him myself, I wondered what the attraction was for my wife. Melvin Johnson looked to me like he could've been a little bit sweet. It wasn't until after I left that I realized he looked just like Prince minus the pants, makeup, and heels. But that wasn't my concern. I just wanted him out of our lives.

In the beginning, before I asked Keisha to leave, I'd decided I needed to try and talk to him, man-to-man.

"You're Melvin Johnson, right?" I asked as soon as the doorman opened the door and let him into the building's lobby.

"Yeah, I am. Who wants to know?" he asked.

"I'm Dexter. Dexter Saintjohn. As in, Keisha's husband," I said.

He looked around the lobby, then at me. "Ah, can we talk about this later?" he asked.

"Naw, we need to talk right now. This is not a social call."

He looked around again. This time he moved over so he could look toward the front door. I had no idea what was going on, but I was there to speak my piece.

"She's not going to leave me," I said with confidence.

"I know," he said. "At first I didn't want her to," he admitted.

"At first?"

"I don't know what we're going to do," Melvin said. "I'm changing my life for her."

"Look, I'm not here to compromise with you," I heard my voice echoing in the lobby. The doorman looked over at us and raised a bushy eyebrow.

"Mr. Johnson?" Melvin looked at the doorman. "Is everything okay?" the older man asked.

Melvin quickly nodded in his direction, then turned back to me. "I think we need to talk about this some other time," he glanced toward the front door again before looking back at me. He couldn't stand still. I wasn't sure if he thought I was going to hit him, but he continued to fidget and move around.

"I'm not going anywhere until you understand what I'm trying to tell you—"

Before I could finish my threat, a tall woman walked in the front door. She was attractive, despite the eyes that said she had been crying.

Melvin looked at her, then back at me. "Ah, I really need to go," he mumbled, and tried to walk in front of me to intercept the woman. She looked over his shoulder at me. I couldn't hear what they were saying. But I was determined not to leave just yet.

"We're not done talking," I said.

The woman stepped away from Melvin and toward me.

"Who is this?" she asked.

I looked at Melvin. His eyes appeared to be begging me for compassion. I chuckled.

"Who am I?" I asked her. Behind her back, Melvin shook his head, staring at me with pleading eyes. He even had his hands clasped as if he was praying.

"I'm Dexter Saintjohn. Your friend there has been having an affair with my wife."

She spun around to him. "What?"

"Wait, I can explain," Melvin cried.

I had mixed emotions when I left Melvin's. I couldn't believe he had a woman of his own but was still trying to lure Keisha away.

In my car, I took a call from Mama. I found it odd that she was desperate to know where I was. She told me she finally understood what I had been trying to say.

She didn't agree with how I felt about Keisha, but she would try to respect the fact that I loved my wife and that I was staying in my marriage.

"Is that what is going to make you truly happy, son?"

"It is, Mama. Keisha is my soul mate," I said.

"I hope she one day realizes just what she has in you, son. I did do a good job. It takes a true man to forgive another," she said.

"I know, Mama. I know. Now let me get home to my wife."

The ringing phone brought me back to my empty home. I still felt like a fool, thinking about how confident I was when I left my wife's lover. I just knew we were on the road to rebuilding our life.

Now, looking around the empty house, I wondered

what was next for us. When I answered the phone and heard her voice, I started thinking again about all I had done to save my marriage and how she had been sabotaging my efforts all along.

I didn't hesitate to place the phone back in its cradle. I wasn't ready to deal with her. I know what Dr. Davidson would've said, but I just couldn't bring myself to think about picking up the pieces of our crumbled marriage.

Keisha

I finally went back to work after a week off. Walking down the halls, I felt like everyone knew my business. They'd smile or say a quick "hello" and I'd feel like they were just testing to see if I'd crack.

I'm not sure how I thought all of these people had found out about my personal life, but I couldn't shake the feeling.

Monday morning a delivery was waiting for me in the teacher's lounge when I took my conference period. It was a plant with flowers and a stuffed animal. A card was included with the delivery. It was from Melvin. I was certain he had sent it before his wife came back.

After reading the card, I became so sick I had to leave early.

I was lying on my bed in the hotel when I pulled the card out again. I planned to burn it, but I needed to hang on to something he had touched for as long as I could. It somehow made me feel closer to him and what we shared before this mess started unraveling.

I was emotionally torn between two men, even though I was alone. If he didn't have a wife, I would've been with him now, after leaving my husband. This was nothing but a big 'ole mess. His letter proved that he wanted me, but he had ruined our chances by not being honest.

> *Dear Lover,*
> *He came to me and said the love he has for you is unconditional, but we're not giving it a fair chance. He also said if I truly cared about you, leaving would be the best thing for us all, especially you. He wanted me to leave you so that you wouldn't have to choose. Everything in me wanted to do what was best for you, but when I tried to picture my life without you it seemed pointless. I know I'm being selfish when it comes to you, but that's only because I've never met anyone like you. If you give to him only a small percentage of what you've given me, I can understand his desperation. But I'm a desperate man too. Because I really do love you, I know I'm no longer playing by the rules but I am going to test our love. In two days I'll leave for Kansas City. When I come back in three weeks if you are waiting in my home I'll know that you feel the same way too.*
> *Signed,*
> *Your Lover*

It took a few weeks for me to realize that my life with Dexter wasn't as bad as I thought. There I was thinking Melvin was the best thing since the sun came up, when he was just somebody else's husband, who probably got bored with being married, just like me, just like I had.

Dexter still wouldn't take my calls. I thought about contacting Dr. Davidson, but chickened out. I have to admit I didn't like being without my husband. Being alone wasn't what bothered me; it was knowing I had probably blown the best thing I ever had. That's what truly bothered me most.

Ironically, I had started praying again. After all I had done, I wasn't sure if God was even interested in hearing from me, but I figured I'd give it a try.

Dexter

I was leaving Dr. Davidson's office when I saw Janet in the parking lot. His office was near her favorite T.J.Maxx store. She walked over to my car before I could get in.

"Dex, what are you doing here?" she asked.

"Oh, nothing much, trying to get my life straight." I shrugged.

Janet leaned against my car, signaling to me that she wasn't about to leave anytime soon.

"People make mistakes, you know," she said casually.

I nodded.

"You know that forgiveness is crucial, right? I mean otherwise, you stay stuck."

There was no way I wanted to break down in front of my sister. I was lonely without Keisha, and over the last few weeks I'd realized how much I had taken her for granted, but still, I had my pride.

"Nobody would look down on you for trying to make your marriage work. I can think of several relationships I gave up on way too soon. You don't want to make the same mistake," she said.

"But sis, she played me. . . ." I shook my head. I couldn't even finish.

"I know it hurts." Janet reached up and touched my shoulder. "I'm not defending what Keisha did, but all I'm saying is when you lose the ability to forgive someone, to me it says you're putting yourself above the rest of us sinners. And I mean, if you've ever even looked at another woman in a wanting way . . . well, let's just say I don't believe any of us are perfect." I swallowed hard and dry and, for a fleeting moment, wondered if they knew what I had done.

"So you're telling me to just overlook everything she did and take her back, just like that?"

Janet didn't answer right away.

"What I'm saying is you have to allow yourself to look beyond the pain, too, to see that you can get past it . . . with or without your wife."

"Has she gotten to you?" I wanted to know. I was shocked by the way she seemed to be speaking up for my wife.

My sister smiled and sashayed toward her car.

"Nobody's perfect Dex, that's all I'm saying. I've forgiven Keisha for hurting you, maybe you should consider doing the same."

"You should," I heard Dr. Davidson say over my shoulder.

I shook my head. "It hurts too bad," I said.

"It does, but you shouldn't stay trapped in pain."

On my way home I thought about what Janet and Dr. Davidson said. I also thought about Keisha and me. I realized our problems may have started when April came back, but they were always lying just beneath the surface waiting for the opportunity to pop up.

Maybe I was just as guilty as Keisha, after all. When I

thought about it, work, the couch, the remote, and even Mama and Janet at times all came before my wife. I knew I was ready for a change, by the time I pulled into our driveway.

This time when the phone rang and I noticed the familiar number, I answered, then sat back to really talk to my wife.

Keisha

Dexter and I were sitting in the living room on a Saturday evening. The news was coming on. Now that I think about it, I never watched the news. It just wasn't something I thought I needed to do.

But this Saturday evening I watched as a news lady was talking about yet another carjacking in Houston. The victim, she said, was 35-year-old Melvin Johnson. He was leaving his downtown loft building when a gunman approached. Witnesses said he resisted and was shot once in his left temple.

That couldn't be my Melvin, there was no way. I felt Dexter staring at me. He must've been looking for my reaction. But all I wanted to know was Melvin's condition.

I couldn't help myself. Tears started rolling down my cheeks and I didn't even move to wipe them. How could they not say whether he had survived?

Just before the news lady switched stories, my cell phone rang. Dexter still sat watching. He didn't say anything.

"Aren't you going to get that?" he asked.

He had no idea how much I wanted to bolt from our house. I didn't want to leave my husband—we had been in counseling for months now and things were getting better—but I needed to know about Melvin.

I hadn't spoken to him since the fight in the hall with his wife. Since then, April had told me bits and pieces about his life. She said he and his wife didn't get back together, and he had even asked about me. She wondered if I ever regretted my decision to stay with my husband. I told her I didn't.

By the time I was finally able to answer the phone, the news had switched to sports. "Hello?" I said stepping away from the family room.

It was April.

"Did you see the news?" she asked.

"I did, but not everything," I replied.

She started crying. I knew I couldn't make any sudden outbursts because I didn't want Dexter to know I was talking about Melvin. I needed April to tell me if Melvin was going to be okay.

"What do you want me to do?" she asked.

"Something!" I said.

"Robert is on his way over to the hospital. I told him I'd call you. I wish you could come out, but I know you can't. I'll try to call Robert and see if he knows anything else."

April never called back that night. I knew nothing more than the fact that Melvin had been shot during an attempted carjacking. He could've been dead, for all I knew.

I had no desire to sleep. The night felt excessively long and lonely. Each time I went into a different room, Dexter found his way there. He never said anything, but he kept a close eye on me.

I lay in bed staring into the darkness for hours as Dexter slept. I mourned my former lover with my husband inches away.

I thought about sneaking out of bed to call and see what happened to the updates I was supposed to get from April, but I couldn't bring myself to do it. I was supposed to be focusing on my marriage, not the man who almost cost me everything.

Later, I found out that the hospital would not release any information about Melvin's condition because of the fact that he was shot during a carjacking and the suspect had not been caught.

When I returned from school, Dexter greeted me at the door. The gloom that once hung over our house after the affair was revealed was gone.

"Keisha, I love you," he said.

Before I could respond or react, he took me into his arms and kissed me passionately. I felt myself submitting to him completely.

I cried as he picked me up and took me into our bedroom. My husband loved me like he never had before. When he exploded inside of me, I knew I had made the right decision to stay. I loved my husband.

In the heat of our passion, he looked deep into my eyes and said, "I forgive you. I just wanted to say it so that you know. I forgive you."

I kissed him with everything in me. I couldn't understand how he found it in his heart to forgive me, but I believed him. And I felt joy. I felt so good about having his forgiveness, even though I knew I hadn't earned it yet.

"How could you know that you've forgiven me? How could you?" I asked.

"Because you're my wife, and when I took a vow to love you, I meant it. You made a mistake, I've made mistakes too, but those mistakes don't have to become you or us. I forgive you because I love you unconditionally." He took my hand and placed it over his chest. "Feel that?" he asked after my palm sat on his chest for a few seconds.

"You have my heart, Keisha."

I wanted to work hard to make sure I took care of his heart; breaking it again was simply not an option this time.

About one month after Dexter and I started seeing Dr. Davidson again I got a phone call from April. It seemed she had finally hooked husband number four. She said Robert decided they should go to Vegas and do it fast and simple. And that's exactly what they did.

I also learned that Melvin did survive the shooting. His sister and mother moved him to a rehabilitation home back in New Jersey where they lived. I felt at peace, knowing he'd have someone who loved him to care for him and be by his side. I didn't have the courage to call and check on him. I thought it was best if I remained focused on my marriage.

It was Christmas Eve, and Dexter and I were discussing whether to top our tree with a star or a black angel. I told him if he didn't make a decision soon, I'd handle it myself.

When I tried to move toward the stepladder, he grabbed me by the waist.

"If you think I'm going to allow my pregnant wife to climb a ladder, you must be crazy."

It had been three weeks since we found out I was two months pregnant. It was Dexter's idea to even go to the doctor's office because I had been sick too much.

I thought about how much my life had changed since Melvin moved to New Jersey and I had absolutely no way of contacting him. I was just fine with that because it made it easier for me to do right. I had even burned the love letter I'd been holding on to.

Sometimes I marveled at what I had been about to give up. I had never known a man with Dexter's patience, integrity, and love. I believe everything happened for a reason, and I think that year was just our wake-up call. Oddly enough, I believe we both now knew the importance of not taking each other for granted.

Our relationship was stronger than ever. Through counseling and constant communication, we were sure we'd rebuild the trust. The love had always been there and at times when I start to feel bad about what I had done, Dexter takes me into his arms and kisses me.

Now we share the couch together. Since I found out I was pregnant, he insists that I take the couch while he rubs my feet. He's very excited about the baby.

Dexter

One day a few months ago when we were stumbling through the storm, I told myself there would eventually be peace in this house. I believed it, I felt it, and I started working toward it.

Looking around at my pregnant wife fast asleep on the couch, I felt proud, like I had accomplished what I set out to do. My marriage was on its way to recovery, and peace had finally found its home in our house.

Every day was a work in progress for us but it felt so different now that both of us were working together. When I called to tell Mama we were pregnant, she said she already knew.

"A mother has a way of knowing these things," she said.

"Oh really? Well, does a mother know if she's having a grandson or a granddaughter?" I asked.

"Whatever we have, we'll love it to pieces. I'm so thrilled to hear the happiness in your voice," she said. But I was certain the thought of her first grandchild may have just been enough to change her outlook on everything.

"It wasn't easy, but I'm glad Keisha and I finally made it here. To this comfortable place in our marriage," I said.

"Yes, I'm just glad that fellow finally saw the light. People these days . . . I can't believe he was persistent about sleeping with another man's wife, hmm, especially when he had his own," she said.

"Mama, we don't discuss that time in our lives, unless we're talking with Dr. Davidson," I countered. One of the things he told Keisha and me was not to give life to any negative energy. We continue to pray together, leave our past in the past, and move on from there.

"I'm just glad he finally got the message," I said, and I meant it.

"Hmmm. Well, it's unfortunate the message had to be delivered in such a way. But maybe that'll make him think twice before he becomes a home-wrecker again."

"Well, he's no longer my problem," I said.

"I'm glad," she added.

"Where's Janet?" I asked.

"Out with that friend of yours again," Mama snickered.

"Hmm, she and Roger are getting along well? That's great news, Mama." Mama didn't sound too good about the possibility of Janet and Roger, but I wasn't about to start worrying about them.

"Well, I just hope his skirt-chasing days are over. But then again, I'm sure he's got the message by now," Mama said.

"Oh, Mama, sometimes you just have to hope for the best," I said.

"Oh, God, no!" she corrected. "Sometimes when it comes to your children, you'll soon learn, when their happiness is truly on the line, sometimes you've got to *send* a message that's loud and clear."

Sometimes I think about that conversation with Mama. I was glad she didn't start attacking my wife, but I also knew she was probably too busy with Janet now that she was dating Roger to meddle in my marriage. I also think about her comment regarding sending a message and wonder if my mother had something to do with what happened to Melvin. Then I'd say, nah, she's not capable of such evil, she just couldn't be.

Either way, I was just glad to have my life, and my wife, back. These days we're both focusing on us, instead of anything that could possibly lead us astray.